The Last Woman 2

JACQUELINE DRUGA

The Last Woman 2 by Jacqueline Druga
Copyright © 2018 Jacqueline Druga

Originally self-published by Jacqueline Druga in 2015
Published by Vulpine Press in the United Kingdom in 2018

ISBN: 978-1-83919-235-7

Cover by Claire Wood

www.vulpine-press.com

ACKNOWLEDGMENTS

A very special thanks to Jenny S. and Linda K. for all your help in getting this book ready.

To Franny L., for putting up with all my midnight rambling messages through the tough scenes.

1. FAYE WILLS

All that I was and all that I ever wanted to live for was gone. It slipped from my grasp long before mankind, as I knew it, vanished from the face of the earth. I was not one of the lucky ones; I didn't die. To some that wasn't a bad thing. To me, at the time, death would have been a dream come true. I wanted to die. I wanted to be rid of this godforsaken world months prior to the disease that crushed life into the ground.

I missed it, you know.

I missed the end of the world. Months prior to the sickness named ERDS, everything about my life ended. I experienced what every other person on the earth would face in a matter of months.

Death.

My son, Mark, just on the brink of his driver's test, was driving with my husband and young daughter. A normal afternoon outing, and their innocent lives were taken by a drunk driver battling his own personal heartbreak.

That driver took from me my entire family. In a snap, in a heartbeat, they were gone. From that day in February forward I didn't care. I lost my job, fell into a deep depression and drank my pain into a state of numbness. It never went away; it would just fade out for an evening only to return with a vengeance when I next opened my eyes.

I attempted to take my life. Why would I want to live? I held a gun to my head but didn't have the courage to pull the trigger. I stood on the bridge but couldn't climb over the railing. I took a handful of pills, washed it down with a third of a fifth of bourbon, only to have a neighbor discover me in the nick of time.

While I battled my demons, the world battled a virus that moved stealthily across the globe. I heard of it and didn't think much of it.

I couldn't be so lucky as to fall sick with the flu and die.

My one-way path to death was set, and subconsciously or not I was drinking my way there. I did so all the way to the night in April when, while out with friends, I hit my limit. Too much alcohol in my blood and I not only passed out, I fell into an alcohol-induced coma and was hospitalized.

How ironic that the thing I'd used to try and kill myself with probably aided in saving my life. The oxygen fed into my system probably filtered the virus; my breathing was slow and so was my heart rate, decreasing the rate of infection and the way it infiltrated my blood.

All of this is theory, but my comatose state had a role to play. Despite the fact that I caught the killer virus, I didn't die.

They thought I did.

In fact, they tossed my body into a makeshift mass grave at a football stadium. When I came to, I was in a cloth body bag, snuggled in between corpses, naked and fly-ridden. Blood from my ripped-out IV shunt covered my arm; my legs were nearly glued together from my own bodily functions.

I had been out in that coma for three weeks, then mistaken for dead and left behind for over three days to rot on top of a pile of corpses.

I lived.

Why?

When I stumbled from that stadium I stumbled into a desolate world emptied of life.

No one remained. I was alone. I thought it was a dream, that it wasn't real. But it was. I was a statistic to whoever tossed me in that pile. Number 4723. Not Faye Wills, but a number.

After I got my senses and strength back, I just wanted to make my way home to die. Make my way across the city to my house. End it curled up in my five-year-old daughter's bed.

While I cried at first over the shock of what had happened to the world, a part of me rejoiced. I didn't sob over the death—I sobbed over the silence. To me, the world ended before the ERDS virus claimed its victims, and I was biding my time until I caught up.

All plans sound good at first, and foolproof. But even I, with all my intentions of ending my suffering on earth, wasn't ready to face the prospect of surviving.

After my family had been killed, and while life still thrived around me, I wanted to relinquish it all and join the ones I loved. Leave that putrid, crowded, pain-filled place. Yet, in a blast of irony, in a silent world void of life, suddenly, surprisingly even to me … I found my will to live.

2. DODGE CASH

Thanks to the convenience of cable news channels, I watched the world's demise unfold before my eyes and didn't even realize it. But in the final days, there was no mistaking it.

My life moved onward despite news of the virus and so did my daily routine. I didn't worry much about some sickness; then again, they didn't say much about it. Just that it was highly contagious and, if possible, stay inside.

The fact that it killed everyone that became infected was skipped over. Probably on purpose. If I'd had the responsibility of informing the public about it, I would have left out that tidbit too.

People didn't stop at first, not in America. I mean, hey, that nasty little bug was overseas. We listened to the news but didn't register what it all meant.

One of my employees in my auto shop told me about this conspiracy site and how they had pictures of mass graves in England. I laughed and told him that it was all propaganda and a way to get advertising money.

No flu or bug killed that many. Hell, not even the Spanish Flu had done what the conspiracy site claimed. But the Bubonic plague did. I forgot about that one, and how much damage it did to the world.

Daily news reports would come on. Nothing earth-shattering or anything that consumed the airwaves.

Slowly, it built.

It seemed as if I couldn't change a brake pad without hearing about an infected country. Then it was infected cities.

I took a little bit more notice when the bug showed up on the West Coast. Nothing really changed much for me as the bug began its course. I'd pick up my kids at the ex's house, take them to school and get to my shop, where I'd face a lot full of cars dropped off the night before. I'd assign the cars, do the repairs, clear out the lot sans the few problematic ones and then head home.

My life was routine. Evening takeout or something on the grill no matter what the weather, a cold beer or two. Three nights a week I had my younger kids, and every Monday night a video call to my son at college while we watched wrestling together.

There was no special female in my life because I'd given up on that. My kids, all three, were my life.

Then the virus that had just been a news report became a reality.

Fast, too. The momentum of the flu was unbelievable. Beginning of April it was overseas. On Easter Sunday, April nineteenth, the warning was put out that it was moving rapidly.

Schools were closed that week, and I couldn't register how quickly it consumed my life. Within a day my popular and busy repair shop was suddenly empty. My mechanics called in sick. Then my ex-wife called to tell me she was sick and that my younger two were getting "the fever."

I felt like I was in the novel *I Am Legend*.

Some European flu sweeping its way across the globe, no prejudice against race or age. Streets were empty, except for those rushing to go nowhere and the military trucks rolling down the roads.

I remember calling Tyler, my oldest. He wasn't sick; it was still early in the virus days and he was in another city. I felt helpless and out of control. I was always able to right the wrong, to fix things, but this was something I couldn't mend.

I couldn't make my kids better. By the time they'd caught it, the cold reality of its lethality was known.

There were body bags everywhere on the streets, or corpses wrapped in curtains, blankets, you name it. People tossed out the dead like trash. Trucks came by and picked them up. We were instructed that if we lost anyone, not to keep them in the home but place them outside with some form of identification.

My ex, desperately ill and my kids not much better, begged me to go to an aid station to get medicine for them. Some sort of relief.

I knew it was a gamble. Especially knowing there wasn't any medicine that could save them. Leaving them meant taking a chance of being gone too long.

Having to go into the city was a risk, but my ex begged me. So against my better judgment, I went. I drove across the bridge, only to have to park quite a distance from the aid distribution tent. God, I waited in line for hours. My phone died, and the last time I talked to Melissa, my ex-wife, she was gasping. I had to get home. If she passed away, who would be there for my kids?

The soldiers passing out medication pouches announced they were done for the day. And like in some sort of bad science fiction post-apocalypse film, people began rioting, yelling, pushing and fighting.

Weren't they sick? To me they should have been more concerned about those they'd come there to help. I turned to leave and was shoved back. An innocent bystander, drawn into the mobbing crowd. I just wanted to push my way out. But I suppose because I'm a big guy, I was a target, and I was one of the first arrested and detained. Before I could even comprehend what was happening, I was tossed in county jail.

I thought they'd let me out. But they didn't.

No one came. No due process of the law. The television covered the virus, twenty-four-seven, and all I could do was watch and worry about my kids.

I tried. I fought, pleaded and begged, but no one cared. I was a common criminal and the guards on duty were only concerned with events outside the jail walls.

Couldn't blame them.

There were forty cells in our pod division, or section, of the jail, and none of them were locked. So we moved freely about the unit. I watched as not only the news team grew sick, but those around me in the cells.

By my fourth day there, I knew getting out was impossible. The course of the flu was fast. My poor children were already gone and taken. I wasn't there to hold them or to comfort them. I wasn't there to tell them how much I loved them.

I wasn't there.

Instead, I was a helpless prisoner in a death ward. Every hour, minute, every second of my days was filled with visions of my poor babies. Suffering, needing … reaching for nothing.

It killed me. It broke my heart so badly I felt physical pain.

It didn't take long for silence to take over. When the news stopped, I listened to the city shut down around me. Bridges collapsing, explosions. Then nothing. No cars. No shouting. Nothing. Not even a damn bird squawked.

The television stayed on for another day, showing nothing but an empty chair. The news crew ... dead, I suppose.

By then, everyone around me was either dead or well on their way. No guards showed up to work. The cells were open, yet the pod unit was locked down. No way out of the jail. They stopped bringing in food and I started to ration and hide what little I had left. Of course, no one around me cared. They were too sick.

There was nothing I could do for them. At first, I tried to administer help, water, whatever I could. It didn't work. Eventually, as the numbers of sick overwhelmed me, I just stayed away.

By the time power shut down, three men in my pod unit remained, aside from me. They died shortly after.

After moving the bodies as far away from me as I could, I stayed mainly in the recreation area. The small one-hoop basketball court was open, with high echoing walls and a barred ceiling with no glass. It was air I could breathe and air that didn't reek of death.

The prospect of getting out of there was dire. I tried everything I could. I could not get out.

I was convinced when the last of my food ran out, I would just die. Suicide wasn't my thing; I'd wait it out until I was taken.

I'd lived my life the best way I knew how. Always tried to be good and never mean. Treat people the right way. Within my soul, I carried that. Despite what had happened around me, I was positive that I'd done all I could.

My destiny was to die and rot in that concrete hell. A broken and crushed man. I accepted that. Until one day, from nowhere, echoing across the empty city, I heard that squeaky wheel.

3. FAYE

To some, waking up to find yourself the last person on earth, or at least believing that, would be a mental trauma. For some reason, it didn't bother me. I was on a course for answers as to what had happened, and then, once satisfied, I'd end my life.

Perhaps my attitude played a factor in wanting to leave Dodge behind when we met. I had no intention of traveling with him. He was filled with hope despite the dire circumstances.

Having been in jail, left to die, Dodge was grateful when I helped him, and clear about the debt he owed. I just wanted to wander off alone to my home. However, I was glad for Dodge. More than I knew, I wasn't physically ready for any journey. He was the crutch I needed. He was strong and safe and he thought ahead.

Me, if left alone, had I made it home, I doubt I would have done what he did. He raided the neighboring homes for food, thought ahead about going south, planned for that journey and searched for survivors. If he and I were alive, so were others.

I didn't care.

He did. He found them.

A gift I would eventually appreciate. We found George and Darie, brothers who had survived. Nine and five years old. They were a focus and a chance to feel needed, for both me and Dodge.

What I didn't realize was that all of it was attacking me, invading my heart, and I wasn't aware of it.

I wasn't alone anymore. Even my neighbor, Bud, had survived. Dodge called out on the radio and the airwaves buzzed. People were indeed alive.

Then came news of a survivor camp in Kentucky, so Dodge made plans to go there. The camp was heading to the Florida Panhandle, where there were other survivors as well as research doctors. A pilgrimage leaving in "X" amount of days.

It wasn't for me. Dodge, Bud and the boys left, and it wasn't until they were gone, with the help of a few subtle messages from Dodge, that I realized I wasn't ready to shuck life.

I wasn't ready to give in. Those boys, those sweet little surviving boys, had infiltrated my emotions, and I didn't know it until they were gone.

Dodge did.

When I realized I'd made a mistake and wanted to go to Kentucky, I also realized how Dodge had known that was going to happen.

He had packed the car for me, with extra gas and a map all routed out. Along with a radio. Instructions on a Post-it said channel seven.

My house was my refuge, my sanctity. It held memories of my life and past, yet I left it behind, taking only a few items. Believing one day I would return.

I made the trek of nine hundred miles, running into delays that shoved me hours behind. Chasing the schedule, I knew I was pushing it with the caravan. So I put it to fate. If they were gone, it wasn't meant to be.

When I arrived in Kentucky, the caravan of vehicles was indeed gone.

But fate had played so many roles in my life since my family was killed that it only seemed to reason it would chime in again.

As I dropped to my knees in defeat, a voice called out to me. A young voice, male; he too had missed the caravan.

Not only was it fate that he was there, it was fate that I had made contact once with the same boy over the airwaves. I was the one who had told him about the caravan to Kentucky.

There he was. I decided he and I would find that caravan.

And if I didn't believe in fate beforehand, my final declaration of faith came when I found out the boy's name. It was Tyler. And not just Tyler. It was Tyler Cash—Dodge's son.

4. DODGE

Admittedly, I was on a roller coaster of emotions and thoughts from the second we left Faye's house. Tucked away in an aging RV called Fastball, we hadn't rolled more than twenty miles and I was looking at that radio.

Call, Faye, call.

She didn't. We were supposed to radio her, but we hadn't heard anything; we all figured Faye wasn't coming. Or worse, she was dead. She'd checked out. The boys didn't know. For all Darie and George were aware, Faye was leery about being the only woman.

"Good thing she didn't come," George said when we arrived in Kentucky. "Ain't no women here. Guess she'll come when we find more women."

There was a gate with one man standing post. He welcomed us. The radio voice we had become familiar with didn't live on base, but a mile away.

Faye had said she was worried that it was bad, that it was all a trap. No way, no how, was it a trap, and I knew it when we arrived.

A man named Sergeant Stockard—or Len, as he asked us to call him—met us when we pulled over.

"Man, am I glad to see you guys," he said, greeting us with a welcoming embrace, like an old friend.

Len had pulled it together. He was on an aid station post until the very end, and he had gathered those who had survived. He double checked the dead, because some of them were only in comas and had been left behind, left for dead like Faye and Darie.

"We have seventy-three survivors, not including you guys," he told me as he showed me around.

They were packing up, getting trucks ready. Using gas pumps powered by generators, like the one I had made, so they could siphon gas from the powerless fuel stations.

"We made contact with the other camp a few weeks ago. Not long after everything died out," Len explained. "A CDC doctor who was testing immunity started gathering people."

"How many are in the Panhandle?"

"Hundreds, I think. They got scientists. Which, you know, scares me."

"Why's that?"

"You have scientists involved somewhere, at least in my opinion, the human factor is gonna get lost."

"So why join them?"

"They sound like they have the resources, or at least the makings for long-term survival. Gotta think of my survivors here. Because most of them need to go on. We have seventy-three survivors. Twelve adults."

There were children all around. Everywhere you looked in the camp you saw a kid running about, some still toddlers, diapers sagging and swaying in the wind.

But none, not a single one, was female.

"Although, this may be the end of the line," Len said.

I looked at him with curiosity.

"You can't continue the human race without women," he said.

Even though I knew about Faye, I didn't say anything. Not a word about her to Len. "Surely there are women."

"I hope there are," he replied. "But this CDC doctor—Lewis, I think his name is—he said the virus was pretty gender-specific. Almost as if it was designed to be a doomsday virus. End the female population, end the race."

"Wait. So there's not a single female in the Panhandle?"

"Not one. Not that has been found. Dr. Lewis said they are aggressively pursuing the matter. What the hell does that mean? I don't know. Scares me though. But for the sake of the kids, we're heading down there. If there is a future, it's with them."

I looked over at Darie and George, who sat with Bud by the RV, Fastball. I heard George's statement about "no girls" in my head and immediately feared for Faye.

Something made me happy that she hadn't come.

I found myself praying that she hadn't taken her life. That somehow she'd had a change of heart. Because as soon as I heard from her, once I got Bud and the boys settled in Florida, I was gonna find Faye. Then I would make a plan with her.

She was a commodity in a dead world. One I felt the need to protect. I immediately wanted to hightail it north and find her.

She was, by all accounts, to the best of my knowledge, the last woman.

I kept my mouth shut, even told the boys to not say a word about her. Bud and I discussed it. Bud was wise; of course, he had been living on the earth decades longer than me, so he had that reliable gut instinct. "If she isn't dead," he said that night, after the boys went to sleep, "then you need to find her and hide her."

"You think she's dead?" I asked.

"She had a really tough tragedy, Dodge. I don't know how she survived it. She tried to kill herself a few times. Nothing is holding her here. For her sake, I kind of hope she took the route out. Because if she didn't, it's gonna be an even tougher life."

"Is it responsible though?" I asked. "If she is the last woman, it has to be known."

"Does it?" Bud asked. "What kind of life does that give her? Either one protected or one in danger. Either way she may be nothing but a closed-in experiment, kept away from all. That's not living, Dodge. It's existing. Faye needs to live. She's been doing nothing but existing for months."

I recalled Len's concern over what the scientists had called "aggressive measures." Len was worried, and even relieved that he didn't have a woman at camp. Because if he did, as he'd said, he wasn't sure what he'd do.

It could be a dangerous world for the one and only woman.

I knew this. I listened to Len. I listened to Bud. I heard what they said and I heard my own heart on the matter. I was a smart man, not dumb.

So why did I do it? Excitement, perhaps. Relief?

I should never have done it. But thirty miles into the trip, when my radio crackled and hissed and I heard Faye calling out, I didn't think. I grabbed that radio. In gratefulness and stupidity, I replied.

"Oh my God, Faye," I gushed out. It was so good to hear her, to know she was alive.

"Dodge, I'm on base," she said. "Where are you guys?"

She was on base. She'd changed her mind. Darie and George squealed with delight and Bud gave an approving nod. "About thirty miles away," I said. "We just left there. Faye, I'll pull over." And I did. Right there and then, I jerked the wheel and moved to the side of the highway. "I'm pulling over. Get on 181 South, it's clear. You can't miss me. I'm waiting. We're waiting. And Faye, wait until you see. Wait until you see how many kids there are. It's amazing."

"I'm on my way. And Dodge ..."

"Yeah."

"I have a surprise for you."

"You're a surprise, Faye."

"No, this is better. See you soon. Over."

"Out." I put down the radio but kept looking at it. I was overwhelmed; Faye was not only alive, but close. My heart raced, my mind was jumbled with excitement. I didn't even notice the caravan had stopped. I had every intention of staying on the side of the road.

Then I saw Len. He barreled our way with a look of determination.

"Shit," Bud said. "Bet he heard the radio."

20

I don't know what exactly I was expecting Len to say, but it wasn't anything near what he did.

Opening the driver's door, I'd barely stepped out when Len started raging at me. "Are you insane?" he growled. "Not only did you know of a woman, but you brought her here?" His voice squealed at the end. "Hashman asked if you had a woman."

"I was protecting her. I said no." I honestly believed he was mad because I had lied.

"Yeah, well, hell of a job you're doing now," Len barked. "If you would have said yes then, we would have told you not to come. To hide her. God knows what the south wants with them, or what they'll do. She's the only one, and she's that close?"

My heart raced.

Len said, "She called out. Anyone listening heard her voice and then you saying her name. Anyone searching for a woman is gonna know where to find her. We have no clue what kind of technology remains down south. Hell, they may track her signal."

My eyes closed tightly. "I'll turn around. I'll go. I'll find her."

"Whatever you want to do, that's fine. But get her turned around some way, somehow. And do it now. For her safety—do it now."

It was a huge mistake for Faye in all her feminine glory to have called out over the radio, and an even bigger mistake for me to reply.

Faye was so excited about finding us, about heading our way. I was so excited about her wanting to live that I simply forgot that she'd announced her presence, that she would be a prize those scientists down south were gonna pursue with vigor.

Hating to do it, I took a moment to think. I grabbed our map and checked the route. I lifted the radio. "Faye. Faye, come in."

"Dodge, I'm driving as fast as I can."

"Stop."

"What? Over."

"Stop." I lowered my head to the radio and took a second to think. "You're the last woman, Faye. To be with us is dangerous. I'll find you. Stop. Turn around. Turn off the radio. Take the route back home. If you have to stop, then stop. But stay hidden. I'll find you. Somehow. Just go."

It broke my heart to tell her that. Even more so, her simple reply of "Got it" sent an ache through my chest.

Faye was a smart woman. I felt that she knew what I was saying and would adhere to radio silence.

It was the last I heard from her.

When the caravan moved on, I waited until I was sure no one was lagging back, that no one was waiting to follow me, then turned around.

Me, Bud and the boys would start our journey to find Faye. But I had a feeling we weren't going to be the only ones searching for her.

5. FAYE

My foot hit the brake at the same moment Dodge gave the order for me to stop. Almost as if his voice were connected to my reactions. I set down the radio as if it were acid and, with wide eyes, turned to Tyler.

The car idled. For a moment we were frozen there.

Neither of us said a word, but I could tell by the look on his face that he was thinking the same thing as me. I looked around, in the rear view mirror, then left to right. Suddenly, the world no longer felt vacant. I was acutely aware of my surroundings. I hadn't given a thought to the whole Kentucky trip, whether or not I was safe or being followed.

Now I did.

"You're the last woman?" Tyler asked. "Is that possible?"

"I don't know."

"Oh my God. You can't be seen."

A part of me felt as if three weeks post plague was a little too soon to be worrying about rapists and marauders. "Soon, but not yet," I said. "Maybe in a few months it will be less dangerous."

"From normal people."

"What do you mean?"

"I mean, right now, from a scientific point of view, if you're the last woman, you're vital and they're going to want you. That place down south, they are science based. They'll treat you like an experiment."

"No," I scoffed. "They wouldn't do that."

"Faye, if you were a scientist and there was one man left in the world, what would you do?"

"Try to figure out why he survived."

"Through experimentation."

It was at that point I realized we were still sitting in the middle of the road. While I still wasn't convinced that my life was in any danger, the urgency in Dodge's voice was enough to heighten my awareness and make me turn the car around.

The one thing I didn't want to do was get off course. I needed Dodge to find us, and he was a half hour or so behind.

My plan was to make some distance. Dodge didn't want me using the radio because I sounded female, but he didn't know I wasn't alone. Tyler could call out, and while I wanted with all my heart for Dodge to hear his son's voice, I didn't want anyone else listening to put two and two together and hear how young Tyler sounded.

Another radio call to a man named Dodge, this one by a young-ster, would be too much of a coincidence. Even I had thought he was younger than nineteen when I spoke to him over the radio.

We'd figure out a coded message for Dodge, and hopefully he'd understand it.

In the meantime, as we drove, not only did Tyler practice his deepest voice, he gave me a deeper insight into who he was.

Tyler Cash was a nineteen-year-old, bright, artistic young man. Thin and lanky, but not real tall. His hair was a little long, which was so unlike his father. In fact, he was a complete contrast to the triple-B Dodge. Triple-B meaning bulky, big and bald.

Where Dodge looked like he should be a professional wrestler or a *Mad Max* biker, Tyler looked like he should be playing guitar somewhere in a café.

"Where did you go to school?" I asked him. "I mean, that you were so far away?"

"New York."

"That's impressive. City?"

"Yeah."

"How did you make it out? I mean, we barely made it out of our city after it all."

"When things started getting bad, my roommate suggested we head out. We went to his parents' house. I had plans to get to my dad."

"He said you talked to him."

Tyler nodded. "I did. I wasn't sick. I told him I was leaving the city, and after traffic died down, I'd make my way home. Then I started getting sick, and I called him again."

This made me curious, because Dodge hadn't made mention that Tyler was sick. In fact, he'd been pretty certain his son wasn't.

Tyler continued. "But he didn't answer his phone. I called my stepmother. She sounded so sick, and she said the kids were sick too. My brother and sister." His head lowered some. "My dad wasn't around. He went to get medical supplies."

"He was in jail. Arrested at the aid station," I said. "I found him in jail. The only survivor."

"Was he ever sick?"

I shook my head.

"I was. I thought I was going to die. Josh, my friend, died, then his mom. I was too sick to do anything about his dad. I just crawled into bed. When I woke up, I guess days later, everyone was already dead. I was out of it, kinda weak for a few days, and then I talked to you."

"It's a scary situation to wake up to a dead world. I know. I lived that too."

Tyler exhaled. "I thought I was the last man on earth."

"And I thought I was the last woman."

"Hey, Faye ..." Tyler said. "You are."

"That we know of."

We talked against the miles traveled. I tried my hardest not to convey any worries to the young man. The last thing I wanted him to be concerned about was having to watch out for me.

Dodge would find us soon. I was confident of that. Dodge would think of something. He always did. He planned things out and took things into account.

Except turning around and heading back from Kentucky.

Dodge hadn't thought ahead on that one; therefore, we didn't have the gas or the means to get any from reserves. We sputtered on our last bit of fuel in West Virginia, and pulled over by a sign that indicated a town called Rooster was one mile away. Hoping that Dodge really was only thirty miles or less behind us, we placed a riddled radio call we hoped he'd decipher.

6. DODGE

The last thing I wanted to do was pull over again. We'd used our last can of gas, and not only did we have to take out the small generator, but we had to open the reserve at the Zoom gas station. We lost valuable time and miles.

I picked up the pace as best as I could in the RV, while Bud read the map. His square reading glasses perched on the bridge of his nose.

"Gotta be on the route," he said. "Has to be."

"So you don't see it?"

"Well, hell, I'm trying—the eyes aren't the best. Give me a second."

I replayed in my mind what the stranger had said on the radio. His voice was deep and he sounded like he was a big guy. He'd called out for Bud.

"Looking for Bud Doyle. Hey, Bud, me and Wills aren't making it. Ran out of fuel in Westie. Sorry we missed the convoy. Hope we can meet up. Right now we're stuck in Westie. This is Rooster. Out."

That was all that was said, and they didn't respond to any further radio calls.

"Wills is Faye's last name," Bud said. "They didn't want to give it away that it was Faye. Westie has got to be West Virginia or a town in West Virginia or Kentucky. Taking the same route back, they didn't make it that far, and I'm not seeing anything that looks or sounds like Westie."

"Who is this asshole with her?" I asked. "Where did he come from?"

Bud lifted his head from the map. "You that concerned?"

"Yes. Because if he was with her when I spoke on the radio, he knows she's the last woman. Probably misleading us somewhere."

"I don't think so. She probably met up with him on base, or maybe he's the reason she headed down there. And I think he would have noticed she was a woman way before the radio call."

"You didn't know him or recognize the name?"

"Nope."

"But he called you."

"Faye probably told him to so no one heard a call for you again," Bud said. "Now quiet, so I can look at this map."

"It's times like these I miss the Internet."

"Yeah, well, it's times like these I'm glad I didn't use it all that much."

I drove with one hand and rubbed my temple with the other. I wanted to look at that map, but didn't want to stop again.

Darie was asleep and battling motion sickness. He was such a good kid. His brother, on the other hand, was a road trip nightmare. George wouldn't sit still. He was like an overbearing, nagging mother in a nine-year-old's body.

"We gonna find her, Dodge?" George asked, poking his head between the two front seats.

"Yes."

"We have to find her."

"Please sit down."

"We have to find her," he repeated, ignoring my request.

"We will."

"She can't be out there. It's got to be scary for her. She is the last woman."

"I know," I said, staring ahead.

"Who is the guy?"

"Please sit down."

"He sounded mean. Think he's bigger than you, Dodge?"

"I don't know."

"You're a big guy. If he's bigger, I'd be scared. I hope she's safe with him. You called him a bad name so you might be scared too."

"Please," I said, stronger. "Sit down."

"Why? 'Cause of seatbelt laws? Can't have seatbelt laws. There's no more police."

"It's still very dangerous." In my peripheral vision I saw him move, but he didn't step back; he shifted to peer over Bud's shoulder. "Why aren't you listening?"

"I wanna help."

"Bud is doing fine. He's looking for a town."

"What town?" George asked.

"We think the man left a clue in his radio call," I said. "Like a secret message giving their whereabouts. We're just trying to determine what town."

"Like here?" George pointed to the map.

"I'll be damned." Bud smiled. "I think the boy is right."

"What?" I asked.

"Rooster," Bud said. "Rooster, West Virginia, and it's about twenty miles from here on this route. That's where they're at. The guy said Rooster."

"Well, I hope you're right," I said. "And good job, George."

"Thanks," he replied brightly. "Now can I stay here?"

"No." I smiled when he whined and moved back.

I prayed that the minds of the nine-year-old boy and eighty-year-old man were right. Because mine was clouded with worry about Faye and this gruff-sounding stranger that was with her.

I picked up the speed on the nearly empty road, and sure enough, twenty miles down, parked by a sign that read "Rooster: One Mile," was the car I'd left for Faye. It was positioned partly off the road, like most abandoned cars. My heart thumped once in my chest then sank to my gut. Immediately I was fearful that this stranger had taken Faye and was playing games with us.

I pulled over, instructing Bud and the kids to stay back as I exited the RV.

More than anything I wanted to call out her name, but again, I was too scared someone would hear. I stepped to the car, hearing the rustling of leaves. I pulled out the pistol from the back of my jeans and walked around the car.

I listened, watching the leaves move in the thick brush.

Then I quickly lowered my weapon, tucked it back in my jeans and exhaled hard with relief as Faye stepped from the foliage.

"Oh my God." I rushed to her. "You're alright."

"I'm fine. I was hiding until you got here."

Reaching out for Faye, I just wanted to embrace her in gratefulness, but she gave me the brush off. A quick acquaintance-style hug that made me step back. When I did, I noticed the smile on her face.

"What's going on?" I asked. "Where's this guy?"

"Not just any guy, Dodge. Look who I ran into on my way to the convoy." Faye sidestepped and the bushes parted.

They had been practicing; it was obvious, providing a heart-stopping reveal that knocked me off balance. I couldn't breathe, I couldn't move. My eyes widened, and I breathed out what air I had left in my lungs.

I did not expect to see my oldest son standing before me.

He cried out a heart-wrenching "Dad!" and ran to me, slamming his chest against mine. I wrapped my arms so tight around him, lifting him from his feet and planting my lips to his cheek. "You're alive. You're alive."

Embracing Tyler, I opened my eyes and made contact with Faye.

From what I had known of her, she was withdrawn. She showed a cold and often emotionless exterior. Drowned her emotions in a bottle of whiskey to keep them in check. To not let anyone know she felt, or that she could feel.

But the Faye that stood on the side of the road showed me her human side. Even if only for a brief moment, I saw the twinkle in her tear-filled eyes. She was happy for me; she was overwrought with emotions.

I broke the embrace with Tyler for a second, placing my hands on his cheeks and staring deeply into his eyes. "I am so grateful to God that you are alive. So grateful. How … How did this happen?"

Tyler turned and pointed to Faye.

"I didn't know," Faye said, lifting her hands. "Remember the boy I spoke to on the radio and told to go to Kentucky?"

"You?" I asked Tyler.

"Yeah, me. But I got there too late. So did she."

"This is fate." I shook my head in disbelief. "It has to be fate. If you hadn't stayed behind, Faye, I wouldn't have my son."

"Yeah, well." She shrugged. "If you hadn't taken everything from my house to piss me off …"

"Whatever the reason," I said, "we're all together. It's the way it should be."

"What about going south?" Faye asked. "The boys …"

"The boys will deal. I can't go there without you, Faye. You saved my life—twice now." I glanced at Tyler. "We stick together on this thing and figure it out."

"What's the plan?" Faye said. "You always have a plan."

"We stop. We regroup. We think. That's what we do first. Figure out our obstacles and go from there."

My son asked, "Where're we gonna stop?"

With a chuckle I looked at the sign. "Rooster seems as good a place as any."

After unloading everything from Faye's car, we all got in Fastball, intentions set on a temporary halt in Rooster. Who knew what the small town held. At least I knew it was remote enough to hide out in until I came up with a viable plan.

THE VOICE OF UNREASON - DR. BARRY CHATHAM

It is completely irresponsible, not to mention detrimental to the human race, to possibly be the only remaining member of one sex of a species, then run and hide. A move not charged by the need for safety but rather one that is selfishly motivated.

The ERDS virus took a lot from this world, and no doubt, it will take the remaining civility. A person left to their own resources is a victim waiting to happen.

A woman is a prize waiting to be collected.

Out in the world, she is a target. In a facility, she is a preserved treasure. We know this.

While the virus wasn't prejudiced against anyone, it did aggressively seek the female population. As a geneticist I was called in early during the ERDS epidemic to find an answer as to why women were struck first. I never did. Even though the virus took months to reach the point where it rippled out of control, there just wasn't enough time.

There was a slim immunity factor, one not found in a single woman. There was also a revival factor of twenty percent.

Twenty percent. However, that revival or recovery happened days after the body was mistakenly pronounced dead. Overcrowded medical facilities, families rushing to remove the deceased from their homes. Whatever the reason, people were buried and burned before they awoke from the ERDS coma.

Complicating matters was the fact that we lived in a world obsessed with the rising dead. They were shooting the survivors in fear of being eaten. What stupidity.

How many of those who rose were women? We'll never know. I have not seen one—alive, that is—in over a month.

By the time the two remaining doctors found a cure for ERDS, it was too late. It was over. The world had fallen apart. But preparations were made in advance for the continuity of the human race. A nice little sector set up and stocked, rapidly erected in the Florida Panhandle.

What a joke.

To have continuity of the human race, you have to have the means to reproduce.

To tell someone who could be the last woman on earth to run is inconceivable to me. A woman who, by the sound of her voice on the radio, was probably younger than forty, still well within the range of child-bearing years. This woman, unless medically altered, could produce a single ovum that could change the current course of mankind.

Who needs the ovum—we have the DNA.

Yet for some reason, she vanishes over the airwaves and is currently somewhere in a country so big, searching for her would be like finding a needle in a haystack.

Whoever this Dodge was, we know he was coming out of Kentucky and that the female was on her way from the same original location.

He informed her to "head back home." Where home was, we didn't know. It could have been anywhere. Though my experts insist it couldn't be more than seven hundred miles from Central City, Kentucky. It just wasn't feasible for the radio signal to have ranged any farther.

People are arriving daily here in the Panhandle. Since we opened the camp and sent out the call for survivors, many have shown up. We will eventually be able to rebuild a part of civilization, produce food and live. Despite our increasing population, it will only ever grow by the number of survivors that come to us.

Without hope of growth, with the possibility of extinction, I fear what will become of those who survive. Will they care enough to be human when they are all that's left of the human race?

In reality, as long as there is a woman, there is hope the race will not end.

We know of at least one.

I am not giving up on that hope.

We have the manpower and resources to send out search parties and actively look for women. We will do that. We have to. In addition, once the Kentucky convoy arrives, we'll learn more about this Dodge and where he originated from, and then we will locate the needle in the haystack. It is a must, and we will do it at any cost. Our lives, our world, our existence, depend upon it.

7. FAYE

When I first saw the sign—"Welcome to Rooster. Population 672"—visions of the Andy Griffith show danced in my head. I foresaw a quaint town square with a few shops, where park benches decorated the sidewalks. The same benches that old men would be sitting on, reading the paper and talking. Bud said that the rural areas may have been spared.

But none of that was the case. None of our fantasy scenarios held true. Rooster was nothing more than a highway strip town, with some frame houses, a gas station and a Wendy's fast food restaurant.

It wasn't an optimal place to stop and park, nor even to hide out.

There wasn't a person to be seen, and unlike everywhere else, we only spotted a couple bodies placed by the trash.

Dodge pulled the RV over directly in front of Wendy's. It was tough, explaining to Darie why we weren't getting chicken nuggets and fries. Dodge tried to pacify the young boy by telling him, "We'll make them for you."

That didn't go over too well for George, who countered, "How? How you gonna make them? They're all processed meat. It went all bad. You can't recreate processed meat, can you?"

Dodge looked over his shoulder with an expression of utter aggravation. "Why do you have to be like this?"

"Why are you misleading my brother? He loves chicken nuggets."

The back and forth between the grown man and the child made me smile. Tyler, on the other hand, laughed. He told us it was quite an accomplishment to get under his father's skin, since his dad was rarely ruffled.

It was unanimously decided that we'd keep moving for a little while. We topped off the tank and canisters at the Rooster gas station and veered from course. Bud had spotted another small town on the map. It was off the main highway, and we set our sights there.

"At the very least," Bud said, "it has lots of green around it. We can camp out there until morning. Make it home then."

Was that the plan? To just make it home? Or were we running? Hiding? All of the above? Nothing was really said, and no plans set in stone. This was unusual, because Dodge was always thinking ahead.

Maybe he just wasn't saying anything.

For certain, he didn't bring up the subject of me being the only woman. That had got buried somewhere. He didn't mention it, and neither did I. The subject would have to be broached eventually. I would wager on that.

Until then, I was content just moving forward.

8. DODGE

There was something about having my son back that made me a big old sap. I couldn't walk by him without touching or kissing him. I think I kissed him more in four hours than I had in the last four years.

It was pure, unadulterated gratefulness. My kid was alive. I was blessed. Yes, I'd lost, but I hadn't lost it all.

My heart was still aching for the two children who were gone, yet I rejoiced in what I still had.

Not to mention, he was pretty good with George and Darie.

Hanover was a perfect stop for the day and evening. We drove for a while down a two-lane, tree-lined road that was barely wide enough for the RV. Then, all of a sudden, there was Hanover.

A town six blocks long and six blocks wide, it looked like an old mining town or something. Simple houses and a few modern trailers. There was a small store, and a few other localized businesses.

There were no people.

I admit, I'd held out hope that this buried little gem would have some folks. It didn't.

We parked next to the fire station, which was located by the smallest community park I had ever seen. The RV fit nicely right by a set of four picnic benches.

Tyler offered to stay behind while Faye and I went out for supplies. I wanted to scavenge that fire department for some first aid stuff and then hit the small store. Seeing how much remained would tell us what had happened in the town, or at least give us an idea. Did they all die in their homes? Or did they move on? It was a ghost town.

Plus, I wanted to talk to Faye. We hadn't had a chance to yet. Last I saw her, I was begging her to come to Kentucky and she was adamant about staying behind to die. Curl up in her daughter's bed and down a bottle of pills.

She said my taking everything was her inspiration to find me. I accepted that. But I wanted to know where she was emotionally and mentally. Was it a passing phase, or was she really on her way to healing? She was months ahead of us all in her stages of grief.

We raided what we could from the fire station and headed to Gluck's General Store. It was funny—because the town was so empty, so silent, we could hear the boys' laughter even though they were blocks away.

As we entered the grocer's, I said, "What made you change your mind and come?"

"Oh, look—across the street, a liquor store."

"Why doesn't it surprise me that you spotted that?"

Faye smiled.

She smiled?

It wasn't a big smile, more a closed-mouth glance. Then she reached for a can of Spam.

"We don't need Spam."

"It's turkey Spam." She held it up.

"Faye, come on."

"Why is it important?"

"I need to know what made you come to Kentucky. I need to know if I'm gonna be finding myself trying to convince you to stay with us."

She looked down at the Spam and then at me. "I had a choice. I chose to live. Can we leave it at that?"

"Noted."

She placed the can back on the shelf and turned to walk away. I took it back, figuring she'd grabbed it for a reason and not just as a means to change the subject.

We ate the Spam with our meal later—it wasn't bad. When evening set in I built a small fire, as the nights were chilly. Bud went to bed early, claiming he was tired. I accepted that. It had been a long day.

Faye stayed outside while I did a quick inventory of what we had. A continuous popping sound carried to me even though I was in the RV. The boys were playing the game Trouble, laughing. It was late, and I debated telling them it was time for bed.

The inventory surprised me. We didn't have as much as I'd thought or hoped. For the short term it was fine, but it wouldn't last. Without a doubt, we needed a long-term plan all the way around.

I grabbed a pack of honey-flavored flat breakfast biscuits and stepped outside. It was the least-eaten food; the boys cringed over them, but I liked them. They reminded me of the oat cookies we'd had when I was in the service.

The boys were still playing their game. Tyler was trying to teach Darie to count spaces, and they were laughing. To look at them, it didn't seem as if they faced the end of existence. It didn't seem that civilization had caught a bug and vanished. They were three young males blocking out the world and playing a board game.

For the moment, life was a camping trip.

I suppose, with all they'd been through, shutting out the tragedy was a good thing.

Faye was seated in a lawn chair at the edge of the RV, a small distance from the kids, but she was watching them. She wore some sort of pink cardigan sweater that looked as if it were hand knitted and had belonged to someone thirty years older.

There was a bottle of red wine on the ground next to her, and it was mostly full. To my surprise, she was sipping from the glass in her hand, not downing the hard stuff.

There was an empty chair next to her, almost as if she were expecting me to sit. I did.

"Hey," I said as I made myself comfortable.

"Hey." She bent forward, picked up one of those plastic cocktail glasses and handed it to me. "The wine is made locally. It's awesome." She poured some into the glass.

"Local wine from West Virginia?" I asked.

"Yeah, I think it's made in a man named Bob's basement. But it's still good."

"Thanks." I showed her one of the honey biscuits. "Cookie?"

"Nah."

"Nice sweater. Did you bring it?"

"No, it was in the lost and found box at the fire station. I keep wondering what fireman lost it," she said in all seriousness. "Bet he looked real cute."

Something about her at that moment struck me. "Did you just make a joke?" I asked.

"I did." She nodded. "Sorry if it was bad."

"It was the greatest joke I've heard in a while. You, Faye, made a joke. You're smiling."

She lowered her head and sipped her wine, then cupped the glass and stared out toward the boys, biting her lip. "I woke up so angry with you. I mean … I went to make coffee, and I couldn't. Everywhere I turned, you'd taken something that was mine."

I tried not to laugh, but a huff of air escaped me.

"All I did was curse you. Anger—and I grew angrier when I thought you did it on purpose because you were thinking, 'oh, she's gonna die and won't need it.'"

"That wasn't why I took the stuff. I took it to make you mad."

"Mad enough to want to find you and yell?" she asked. "Let me tell you something, Dodge. In the middle of that anger, I realized … I was feeling. For the first time in almost four months since my family was killed, I felt something other than self-pity or numbness. That anger, no matter how intense, reminded me that I was alive. And the toy that Darie left. I was missing the signs. And then I just took off before I missed you guys completely."

"I'm glad you did, and glad you were late, because I wouldn't have found my son."

Faye tucked her hair behind her ear. "He's a good kid, and I am so happy for you. Seeing him. Seeing George and Darie. Not all lives were ripped apart."

"We're gonna do this, Faye. You know that, right?"

"Do what?"

"Survive. Live." I finally tasted the homemade wine. "This is pretty good."

"See? I told you." She paused. "And I hope you're right. We just need a plan."

"Well, I kind of have a plan." I winked.

"I knew it."

"I just thought of it though. I think we head back home. We're all from the same area. Go home. Adjust. Absorb and heal. We scavenge what we can. The farm crops will be growing soon, so we can raid those. Get enough ready for the winter and then head out."

"Where?"

"South or west. We'll figure it out. A place we can eventually plant our own food which has access to fresh water. Wells, maybe. Somewhere we can be secluded and safe."

"Secluded and safe, huh?" She breathed out. "To keep me hidden."

"Not hidden. Just safe. I don't ever want you to feel like you're hiding."

"I can't be the last, Dodge. I can't," she said, desperation clear in her voice.

"I don't think you are," I said. "But I can't take that chance."

"I don't expect you to take on that responsibility. I don't want you to have to feel that kind of pressure."

"We're in this together, Faye. All of us. Fate brought us together for a reason. I'm not taking on anything I can't handle. Except"—I finished the glass of wine—"this stuff. It's a little potent."

"Yeah, hence why I said sip." She refreshed my glass.

"It's getting late. Should I get the kids down?"

"No." Faye shook her head, still watching them. "They look so happy. Look at them."

I did. The kids laughed and set up for another game.

"They're forgetting the world right now," she said, "and I envy that. So I think, if you don't mind, I wanna live vicariously through them for a moment."

"Sit here and watch them?"

"Yeah, sit here and watch."

I raised my glass to her. "Life goes on, Faye."

"It does." She clinked her plastic cup to mine. "And for the first time in a while, I'm realizing that."

9. FAYE

It was the first summer without my children, the first time in forever I wasn't running out to the mall for new school clothes. The excitement of the first day of school was gone, because there was no excitement over the first day of summer vacation, or my getting tired of the kids being home all day.

I missed those days of telling them to step away from the television and go out and play, or to put down the video game. Go get fresh air.

"Mom, it's too hot."

I absolutely, positively dreaded the weather really warming up.

From the moment we made it back, Dodge ditched the usage of any radios. Just on the outside chance the people from the CDC had science fiction technology and could zoom in on us.

What Dodge had originally foraged was miniscule in comparison to what the houses that hadn't been touched still contained. The stores that remained were fully stocked, especially in the back loading docks. We had plenty to choose from.

While I didn't hide, I didn't leave my community either. Our housing plan was gated, and that offered a minimal layer of security.

It took about a week for Dodge, Bud and Tyler to remove the bodies from the street and homes close by. That helped with the smell. By one month post ERDS, the worst of the stink had started to subside; just a hint of it lingered. I didn't know if we had just got used to it or if the bodies had decayed enough to stop smelling.

Bud claimed it took about sixty days. His reasoning was, "That's why no one ever smells bodies buried in the woods; eventually they rot enough to not smell as unholy."

George marked a calendar every day, and even started to make the next year's. At first I wished he wouldn't, because he announced the date every day, and yelled out at noon as well.

"It's twelve o'clock." He'd just shout it, diligently winding his superhero watch.

George was our official timekeeper, and I became glad he was.

Because of him I knew it was my daughter's birthday, my anniversary. I was able to mourn the loss and celebrate my chance to have those days.

I was making oatmeal when George got up, announcing, "It's August thirty-first. Boy, we'd be in school. We need school—who's gonna teach us?" He sat at the table.

Dodge produced this "Don't look at me" look, and I was about to volunteer when Tyler said, "I can teach you. I'll be your art teacher. Music too. Faye, bet you are good with numbers."

"Not by my checkbook," I replied. "Reading. I'm good with reading."

"I'll do math," Bud said. "I was a tax attorney. I'm good with that."

History would have to be a group effort, and there were books that would help. After all, the plague hadn't destroyed the pages of old stories that graced the shelves of libraries. We could always get them.

In fact, Bud had already taken to reading books on farming. We'd cultivated our own seedlings, and the tomato plants were amazing. We spent a lot of time drying out the food and readying it for travel.

I thought it was a mistake to leave. We had enough supplies to make it through the winter. But I was outnumbered. The general consensus was that we wouldn't make it through the cold and snowy weather. If we did stay, it would be a challenge, and too much for the little ones to handle.

The three and a half months back at my house were all about preparation. I realized this as the house grew empty and the supplies were moved into our transportation. We would take the RV and a car.

It was unsettling to me, because we hadn't heard anything. We hadn't seen anyone. No one came after me for being the last woman. Perhaps that was over and done with. We just didn't know.

We had no set destination; we were just going to head west then south. That thought scared me, because I had become complacent in my own world, in my own home. I hadn't a clue what lay beyond my housing plan, much less the city.

Soon, we'd find out.

It was particularly cool for the last day of August. I stood by the window, watching Dodge load up the car. A chill swept over me, and I didn't know if it was the breeze or the ominous feeling I had about leaving.

I didn't want to leave. But what choice did I have?

Bud, Dodge and the boys had become a huge part of my life. Without them I was back to nothing, and I wasn't going there again. So my only option was to go where they went.

I just hoped the foreboding feeling that swelled within me was only my fear of the unknown, and not some psychic premonition I was trying to ignore.

10. DODGE

Bud had started smoking cigarettes again. He'd kicked the habit three decades earlier, but since he really didn't care anymore and they were plentiful, he lit one after another. Though I wasn't fully convinced he was actually inhaling.

He loved the idea of mapping out our route into the unknown. He and his wife had taken numerous trips in the RV, so hitting the road was nothing new to him.

He yammered on about which roads we'd take and his ideas for good places to stop. He couldn't wait until daybreak, when we'd roll out on an adventure into uncertainty. His enthusiasm matched that of a kid waiting on Santa. He just wasn't winding down.

My head was still reeling after the daily, post-dinner argument-slash-discussion with Faye. It was the same as always. She didn't want to go. Why did we have to go? As if I were suddenly going to tell her something new and the light would switch on.

Truth was, I had nothing new. We had to go.

The weather was going to play a big role. And despite how secluded the small gated community seemed, it wasn't. More than anything, I wanted to stay back too. It had been months since we'd left the area; we didn't know what the world held for us. Things could have gone really bad.

We just didn't know.

But staying in the open space of that housing community wasn't going to cut it. I knew in my mind what I was searching for as a final destination, or at least a long-term stopping point.

A structure where it was warm, protected and far away from civilization—or rather, former civilization.

Good people had survived, but so had the bad, and chances were those people were emerging, starving, and would hit the cities and the previously populated areas. We couldn't stay; a fire would send a smoke signal to be seen for miles. We couldn't practice shooting because sound traveled. It was such a quiet world; I could be blocks away and still hear Bud cough.

Imagine if someone heard Faye laugh or yell, which she did when the boys were being bad, or to call them in for supper.

We didn't know what to protect ourselves from, because we simply didn't know what was out there. In my mind, staying put, we were sitting ducks waiting for trouble.

I remember a quote from an author named Alan Cohen. "There is more security in the adventurous and exciting, for in movement there is life, and in change there is power."

We were going on an adventure, the excitement was in the unknown, and we would keep moving.

It was the only way to gain power over all that we had lost. To forge ahead and keep going.

As the night dwindled down, I too found myself suffering from pre-travel jitters and decided to take a walk. The moon was pretty bright, and that helped light the street. I wouldn't go far; I just wanted to walk. I was a block from the house when I heard it.

A snap, in the distance. As if something had been stepped on or broken. We hadn't seen or heard any animals, and in the quiet that sound carried and echoed.

I stopped.

I pulled my pistol from my jacket and lifted the flashlight, aiming in the direction of the sound.

I could have sworn I caught a flash of movement between the houses, and my heart started to beat hard. I stood there for the longest time, waiting, watching and ready.

Nothing happened, and I heard no more. I wanted to chalk it up to my imagination, but it wasn't. Someone was there. I saw the movement, heard him, and when the wind blew, I smelled him.

I may have scared him, or he just backed off. In either case, I didn't take any chances. I stayed awake the rest of the night, sitting on Faye's porch. That simple sound, the movement and the whiff of body odor, reiterated what we had to do.

We had to leave. As much as I wanted to find a reason to stay, it was no longer an option. Our little suburban sanctuary had been discovered.

THE GAME CHANGER - MAJOR JAMES REYNOLDS

Basic common sense told us that if the surviving female was indeed at Central City, Kentucky, then she had picked up a radio signal to make her way there.

By all accounts she was at the farthest seven hundred miles from that convoy point. I was in charge of the search and recover mission. Instead of going out wildly, we waited until the CC convoy had arrived and settled, and interviewed several key people.

We learned that the man named Dodge had arrived with one older gentleman and two young males. The female was not with them.

No one remembered a license plate nor recalled asking them where they came from. They were in an RV. One person recalled the older of the boys having a deep southern drawl. The relationship between the older males and younger was connected, which told me they had been together for at least a few weeks.

Since none of the older individuals or the female on the radio had a southern accent, I made the determination that the boys were more than likely discovered in their home state by Dodge and the older man, who had come from a state that had a more northern accent. With the seven-hundred-mile radius in mind, that really left only four—Illinois, Indiana, Ohio and southwestern Pennsylvania.

It was a high priority to locate the surviving female, and I was given all the resources I needed for the mission. I sent out teams to each state, while I ventured out with the Pennsylvania team.

We would comb every square inch if needed and bring in air support only when we narrowed their location down to a smaller radius. Problem was, with each passing day, they were getting farther away. But if it were me, if I were protecting the only woman, I would keep her away from the south until the weather was too much to handle.

We had time.

While the human race had dwindled, nature seemed to have found its niche in the apocalypse. Growth appeared rapidly and in full force, making road travel more tedious on the back roads as trees extended out.

If they did travel, soon they'd leave a trail. But in my mind, they weren't traveling. Not yet.

We were growing weary, and our supplies were dwindling. I sent men back to base for more. I remained behind, the search on hold, with one other man. We were in the camp we had set up just outside a small community in southwestern Pennsylvania when a good breeze swept in and I caught the scent.

Food.

I followed that scent until it stopped, and then I saw a hint of light. It gave me even better guidance. However, when I arrived at what looked like a gated community, the light was gone. Or perhaps it was just further in. I made it inside, and that was when I spotted the male.

He was the only survivor we had seen in months.

He was large in height and bulk, and I wasn't certain if he was alone or if there were more. I did know that when he pulled the weapon, I wasn't taking any chances. My uncertainty of the situation compounded with only one source of backup, I retreated. It wasn't our mission to engage or to make a hostile approach. Coming at the man at night would be sending the wrong message.

I figured the morning would be the best time to check out his camp and see if this was where the surviving female might be hiding. However, when morning came, there was no one there. The man and any companions had slipped out early.

The two of us were able to determine where they had been staying, and oddly enough, on the mailbox perched in front of the picture-perfect suburbian house was the name Wills.

I didn't think anything of it at first, but the soldier with me asked, "Isn't Wills the name used on that radio call we picked up after the female disappeared?"

He was right. It was. We entered the unlocked home to find it void of food, water and photographs. Anything personal had been taken.

But not everything.

A desk drawer in a home office gave us the confirmation. The home belonged to a Faye Wills.

I knew for sure the surviving woman's name was Faye.

We had it. We'd found where they were, or at least where they had been staying up to only a few hours earlier. The house still smelled of food and people.

They couldn't be far; I was one hundred percent certain they were within the near vicinity. Even with their head start, and even though we didn't know which direction they had taken, we had an area. It wouldn't be hard to find them. I was confident we would, and soon. A few hours and we'd lock on.

I radioed base and called for the air team.

11. FAYE

It shouldn't have surprised me one bit that Bud's route to the west would follow a trail of KOA campsites. I found out about it as we were getting into the cars and Bud pulled out a KOA map.

Dodge championed the idea to me after initially questioning it: "We're living camp ground to camp ground?" I hit the phrase "It figures." After all, Bud and his wife had always been on the go in the RV.

It was hard, saying goodbye to my home. When I'd left it months earlier, a part of me felt that I would be back, and I did return—sooner than I'd expected. But this time, as I took one last look at my family home, I knew it was the last time I'd see that house.

Dodge's mood was off. The usually confident man was quiet. Something was on his mind, and he looked tired. I didn't push the issue, figuring we'd have time to talk later.

I could tell, though, that he was deep in thought about something other than our travels. He was squinting a lot, like he had a headache, causing lines to deepen at the sides of his eyes.

When Dodge was in thought, he squinted. Almost as if his eyelids held the answers.

The RV was packed to capacity and so was the compact car that I would drive. We would all take turns behind the wheel. Our travel plans didn't include going too far per day. We weren't really aware what the roads would be like.

The plan was to avoid Kentucky, and more so to avoid going south for a while. Stay clear of the route we'd taken to Central City. We'd simply move west, and then when we hit Illinois, we'd go south. Sometime while I slept, Dodge had come to a decision on where we would head—Louisiana was the first state of choice. Close to the Lake Charles area. Not that Lake Charles was a remote town, but we'd find a place nearby. The weather was warmer there and they had a lot of rain, which would help with the issue of finding fresh water.

I didn't argue, because I didn't know much when it came to long-term survival plans. My argument ended when the decision to leave the house was taken out of my hands—something that, unless proven to me otherwise, I would always have believed was a mistake.

We were moving by sunrise. It felt rushed, but I don't know why.

In my mind, I saw us cruising down the highway without a problem. That wasn't the case.

Since I had missed the final days of civilization, I didn't know that people had run for the hills, trying to get to remote areas to avoid infection. But the government sealed off roads to keep the disease from spreading, and since military personnel were scarce, they'd later taken to destroying them. They had dug or blasted huge, gaping holes right across the highways, in places where you couldn't just drive around.

We saw the first of the road-blocking craters about forty miles into Ohio. There went the idea of heading directly west. I was behind the RV when it slowed down, then finally stopped.

The toy radio hissed, and then Dodge's voice crackled through. "Hey, Wills, we have to turn around."

George, who was my riding partner, lifted the radio. "Roger that."

They were pink princess radios; Dodge got them from the budget store so we could communicate during the ride. He'd figured the range wasn't that good, so we wouldn't be picked up by an unwanted third party. But just on the outside chance, I wasn't allowed to speak on them.

I hung back until Dodge turned the RV. He lifted his hand in a wave as they drove slowly by, and then I turned around and followed.

"Bud said don't worry," Dodge said over the radio. "He said we're in KOA heaven."

I chuckled, and said to George, "Tell him I said 'I bet.'"

"Wills is not surprised," George stated.

I followed—lagged behind, more like it, constantly being told to keep up. Old habits of being a law-abiding driver die hard. After backtracking a good ten miles, we veered off at a lesser-known exit.

"This will take us north," Dodge said. "How you doing on gas?"

George radioed my response. "Still good. But we're getting hungry."

"Oh, stop." I nudged George playfully. "I didn't say that. Are you hungry, though?"

"A little."

"You didn't eat much this morning."

"That's 'cause Dodge kept hurrying us," George said.

"He did, didn't he?"

"You don't suppose he was worried about something, do you?"

George was perceptive, because I had also noticed a difference in Dodge's demeanor. It was a conversation I wasn't going to have with George. So I said, "Nah, he's fine, just nervous. But if you're hungry, I have chips. Want some?"

George nodded quickly and assuredly.

My small bag was in the back seat, and as I reached for it, I glanced through the back window. Coming up behind us, in the distance, were a motorcycle and a car.

"Shit."

"What?" George asked.

I quickly turned around. My hair had grown, and I grabbed it, pulling it upward. "Put your hat on my head. Hurry."

George took off his baseball cap, his little hands shaking as he adjusted the strap. "Someone's coming, ain't they, Faye?"

"Hurry."

He placed the hat on my head while I held my hair. Heart pounding rapidly, I glanced in the mirror at my plain reflection as I gave George instructions. "Radio Dodge. Tell him we may have trouble."

George picked up the pink radio.

12. DODGE

It didn't take long for me to remember why Tyler and I butted heads all the time. In the first few weeks after our reunion, and after the relief at knowing he was alive started to fade, my Tyler reality came forth.

"Tyler," I said, trying not to lose it. My hands on the steering wheel, looking forward, I focused on the empty road while he rambled on incessantly.

"I'm telling you."

"Tyler."

"It was too fast. Bet me. Bet me it was a means of population control."

"Okay." I held up my hand. "Let's say for a second, hypothetically, that it was deliberately released as a means to control the population. Don't you think they would have tested it? Or at least been aware of its lethality? Better yet, if it was population control, don't you think it went a bit far, killing off all the women?"

"They didn't know."

"They would have tested it."

"On who?"

I shrugged. "I don't know."

"Just think about it."

"I do. You bring it up every time you see a picture or a billboard."

"Why are you being mean to me?" Tyler asked. "You always were."

"I'm not being mean. Really."

"I just don't think it was nature."

I huffed, thinking, *Here we go again*, just as the radio hissed out static. Before I could register my happiness at the interruption, before I even heard George's voice, Bud whispered, "Dodge." He sounded worried. I sensed it in the way he said my name, and I immediately glanced up at the mirror.

"We have trouble," said George.

No shit. In the rearview mirror, I saw a motorcycle and a car. We hadn't seen anyone in months. Then again, we hadn't really left the safety of the community around Faye's house.

Seeing people was a bit disconcerting, especially since they seemed to be following us—and then the motorcycle pulled up to Faye's car, drove alongside, and the rider looked in.

I put on my turn signal and slowed down, pulling over. *Stay in the car, Faye. Stay in the car.*

I checked my pistol, securing it within reach, and looked at Tyler. "Go in the back with Darie. I need Bud ready to roll if there's trouble."

"What do they want?" Tyler asked.

"I don't know."

Bud said, "Do you think they saw Faye?"

"She's wearing a hat, but she's not hiding that she's a woman too well." I opened the door and stepped out.

The car pulled up just on the other side of the road, and the motorcyclist parked next to the car. I thought all was good until I noticed Faye pulling close. I tried not to cringe as she parked between us, only about ten feet back.

Was she nuts? She certainly wasn't thinking.

Again, I silently pleaded for her to stay in the car.

There were two men. The one who got out of the car was about my age, the other maybe in his late twenties. Surely there were more. Why would they drive two vehicles if there weren't?

The older of the two seemed hospitable enough as he made his approach. "Hank." He held out his hand. "Boy, it's good to see people. This here is Powell."

Powell kept looking at Faye's car. "Got a little kid in there." He stepped closer to the window.

"Can you not?" I said. He stopped. "I'm a little leery. I mean, we don't know you."

Hank nodded. "Makes sense. Saw you guys ride by our camp. Saw the gasoline cans."

Hank's voice faded to the back of my head; my focus was on Powell, who was still looking at the car. And then the door opened.

Even though Faye kept her distance and was wearing that damn hat, I wanted to scream. What was wrong with her? Why would she get out? I was going to kill her. I readied myself for trouble.

Powell kept staring.

Then, finally, I realized Hank was asking me something.

"I'm sorry, what?" I said.

"Gas. Can you spare any gas?"

"Seriously?" My eyes went back and forth between the two men. If they hadn't seen people in a while, then why were they acting so casually? Something really was up.

"Seriously," Hank said.

"My man, there are gas stations everywhere that have reserves. The reserves are filled."

"There's no power."

"Go to Home Depot, grab a generator and a pump, then suck it out like us."

"Why are you getting so upset?"

"It's just that, this is feeling awfully uncomfortable," I said. "I mean, you follow us, you shake hands and you keep looking at—"

"That a woman?" Powell said. "You got a woman."

There it was.

Powell took two steps toward the car. "Hank, he got that woman the radio called out about."

I reached out and grabbed his arm. "It's not a woman." I made eye contact with him, staring him down, trying my best to look intimidating. After all, I wasn't a small man. It had to work to some degree

"Looks like a woman," Powell said with a snicker.

"It's not."

"I can smell a woman."

I laughed. "You're out of your goddamn mind. Smell a woman. That's a man."

"I'm telling you—"

Hank silenced him. "Powell. If the man says that's not a woman, it's not. Got it?"

"But—"

"Got it?"

"Fine."

At that point I was done and ready to go. I glanced around, looking for more people hiding in the bushes. I shouted to Faye. "Wills. Back in the car, we got to go."

Faye's back was to us; she nodded and got in the car.

"Where you headed?" Hank asked.

"West. Now if you don't mind …" I grabbed the RV door.

"What about that gas?" Hank said. "Looks like you got plenty. How about a can till we get to the Home Depot?"

My jaw twitched as I assessed the men. I was still expecting someone to jump out at us from the side of the road. "Stay here," I instructed, and walked over to the car. I stood by the driver's window and reached up to the roof.

Keeping my voice low, I said, "Don't let on I'm talking to you. But what the hell were you thinking, getting out of the car?"

"I thought you were in trouble," Faye whispered.

"And you would do what?" I undid the chord holding the gas can.

"Why are you giving them our gas?"

"So they go away."

"Will they?"

"I don't know. Shut the window." I pulled down the canister.

"Do I stink?"

My shock at her question made me pause. "What?"

"Stink. That man said he smelled ..."

I didn't even let her finish or justify her comment with an answer. I shook my head and walked back to the two men. "Here, this should start a generator. Saw a sign for a home store about ten miles back. Best of luck to you."

"Much obliged." Hank took the can. "We'll be seeing you."

"I doubt that," I said.

"You never know." Hank smiled and went to their car. "Powell."

Powell hesitated. He was too focused on Faye. He knew. How could he not?

My plan was to wait until they drove off. Once I was satisfied they were moving in the other direction, I'd get back in the RV and we'd carry on to our first night's stop.

But no sooner did Powell move toward his bike and Hank open the driver's door of his car than we all heard it. And then we saw it.

A helicopter.

It flew slowly overhead, circled and then hovered for a moment. The wind from the blades was sharp, tiny particles of dirt blasting against my face.

"Must be looking for that woman," Powell said snidely, then jumped on the bike and started it up.

"See you around." Hank got in the car. Within a minute, they had both turned around and were headed back in the opposite direction— south. They did take one more look into the car as they rode by, which sent a shiver up my spine.

Before getting in the RV, I walked back up to Faye's window. "Don't ever get out of the car again. Please."

"Dodge," George said excitedly. "You see that chopper? They rescuing us?"

"I doubt it," I replied. The chopper was not good news. It had moved on, but I was certain it would be back.

"What did they want?" George asked. "I mean, they were looking at us."

"Yep." I nodded. "Looking for her. Stay"—I pointed—"out of sight."

"Dodge, wait," Faye called as I stepped away.

"What, Faye? And please don't ask me if you stink."

"No, those men. You think they'll follow us?"

"I don't know." I sighed. "They went in the other direction. Let's just hope it stays that way." With a tap to the roof, I walked back to the RV.

I just wanted to get moving. Hopefully the campground would be as remote as Bud kept saying it was.

It had to be.

13. FAYE

A part of me thought Bud was out of his mind and that map of his was too old—until we pulled through the gate. Of course, the hidden paradise campground was marked at its entrance, and Dodge made it a point to pull over and remove the sign.

Dodge was paranoid, unnecessarily. We had encountered that duo, but I didn't see the problem with them—yeah, they were odd, but they weren't dangerous. They'd just needed gas.

I tried to bring it up with Dodge, but he blew me off. I guess he wanted to settle for the night. The campground was really nice, even with the overgrown grass and the empty grounds. The playground was still viable because it didn't have grass, just mulch, and since it was still daylight, the boys ran to the swing set.

Bud told us people had retreated there when the virus hit, and we saw the campers and their tents when we arrived. Some were wrapped up, some just lying on the ground, in and on sleeping bags, their corpses showing signs of the sickness.

Those poor people. They had come to find refuge from the sickness, but were unable to outrun it after all.

Personally, I would have stayed in my own home, my own bed. Not in some pop-up tin can or tent.

Although all the cabins were nice, there was a luxury one in the center of the compound. Bud made a bad joke: "Bet me it's available."

Dodge laughed, and so did George and Darie. Tyler and I sought the humor.

It felt secure there, safe and hidden. There wasn't a soul around, yet Dodge felt the need to go check the grounds. I could only imagine the pressure he was feeling, knowing that he had left the sanctity of my neighborhood and that he had to watch out for me.

My mind began to race with neuroticism. I couldn't shake what that man had said, that he could smell that I was a woman. The fact that it was inane bothered me even more. How could I worry about something so stupid in a dead world? Yet I did. No matter how barren and different life was, a part of me slipped back to the mindset of what it had been like before the virus.

It made me worry more. How could Dodge protect and hide me if someone could catch my scent? The hat and baggy clothes couldn't stop that.

They could only catch my scent if ... I smelled.

That thought made me cringe. I washed, I did. Every chance I had. Granted, full baths were few and far between, but not a part of my body suffered from a lack of cleansing.

Perhaps I was ill, or it was an aftereffect of the sickness.

They all acted like I was crazy; I probably sounded it.

I asked Darie, "Do I smell?"

He giggled and said, "Yes, you smell through your nose.'

"No, Darie, do I ..." I lowered my voice, as if it were a curse word. "Stink?"

He laughed.

I asked George. "You're silly," he replied.

Tyler's response was a question. "Are you worried?"

"Yes."

"That's funny that you're worried about that." And he walked away.

Dodge told me firmly, "There are other things to worry about."

I asked them all, and they all told me I was silly. Yet not a single one of them said, "No, you don't smell."

Bud, I never got to ask. He made it abundantly clear to me that he was not interested in discussing the matter when he told me he was getting the well pumps working and we'd have water soon.

Until the water was ready, I'd keep my distance. I was a bit ashamed.

I sat on the side porch of the cabin by myself, watching the boys until they were done playing and Bud called them for supper. Tyler was off working on some project; I could hear him singing.

I enjoyed listening to him. The sun was just starting to set when Dodge startled me, sitting next to me on the step.

"Hey," he said.

I moved over.

"I brought you dinner. Canned stew." He handed me a bowl.

"Thanks." I moved even more out of his way. "I'll eat in a few minutes." I set the bowl on the step next to me.

"Faye, what in God's name is wrong with you? You never miss eating with the boys."

"Truth?"

"No less."

"I'm a little embarrassed."

"About?"

"The fact that I ... that I smell."

"Oh my God," Dodge said with a gasp. "You cannot be serious?"

"I am, Dodge. I stink."

"Faye …"

"No. I asked, and everyone laughs or says I'm silly, but no one will say I don't stink."

"Is this all still over what that asshole said?"

"Yes." I nodded. "He said he smelled me." I shuddered. "For a woman, that's just horrible to hear."

"You realize the world pretty much went to shit, right?" Dodge said. "People died. Nearly everyone. Worrying about body odor or smelling is absolutely absurd."

I gasped. "So I do stink."

"Stop it."

"You're not answering. That man said he smelled a woman."

"And he probably did."

I hurriedly covered my face.

"The whole goddamn apocalypse can smell you."

I just wanted to die, right there and then.

Dodge continued, only this time with an air of hostility. "You wash, Faye. You wash all the time. You use that stupid purple soap, and that blue powdery-smelling deodorant, not to mention that spray for bugs. It's ridiculous."

"You sound mad."

"It makes me mad. We can cut your hair, dress you bad, hide your breasts, but we can't stop you from smelling like a woman."

"In a good way, not—"

"Faye," he barked. "This is not important. Do you think I care if I smell?"

"No. But in case you're wondering, you don't."

Dodge growled. "Why is this a concern? There's no reason to try to smell good."

"You're wrong," I said. "Everywhere we go, everything smells bad. The world has gone so wrong, and we are reminded not only by what we see, but by what we smell. A good smell is just a tiny deviation that is needed. Also, smells can trigger a memory, good or bad. You smell roses, you may think of your grandmother, or honey and think of a friend. You smell rank body odor, you may think of that boy who beat you up in eighth-grade gym class ..." I paused when Dodge just glared at me. "Not that anyone beat you up in eighth-grade gym."

I playfully nudged him.

Dodge folded his hands, resting his elbows on his knees. "Faye, I like the way you smell. Don't get me wrong, I do. It makes everything wrong with the world a little more tolerable at times. But right now, you're the only one that smells like that, and that worries me. I can't keep you safe if they can lock onto your scent."

I sighed heavily as I realized what he was saying. It wasn't that I was *trying* to smell feminine, it was that the things I was accustomed to using *were* feminine. "I'm sorry. I didn't even think about it."

"Yeah, well, neither did I." Dodge looked at me and gave a tight smile. "Honestly, I didn't until that guy said it, and all of a sudden I noticed the powder smell. And it pissed me off that I missed that. I didn't even think of it. That won't happen again."

"Dodge, you don't have to do this. You don't have to stress out to keep me safe. I am not your responsibility."

"I know I don't have to do anything. It's what I want to do." Then Dodge did something odd. He reached over, and out of the blue, yet so naturally, he rested his hand on mine. "I just want you to feel safe, that's all."

I looked down at his hand, felt the roughness of his skin. Then, as I felt the security of that hand, I slipped my fingers in between his. "More than you realize, I do. I feel very safe."

Dodge smiled and chuckled, almost nervously. He stared at me for a second, then brought our joined hands to his lips and kissed the back of my fingers before releasing his hold. "Good." He cleared his throat. "And now that we've established that you don't stink …" He reached over me and grabbed the bowl of food, then placed it in my hands. "Eat."

I laughed. Not loudly, but an airy laugh that escaped my chest. I enjoyed that moment on the steps with Dodge, and then I enjoyed my canned stew.

14. DODGE

The helicopter made three passes around the camp, waking me up just after dawn. I didn't get too much sleep, but I managed more than I did the night before.

Tyler was on watch. He'd said he'd stay up all night and sleep in the RV during the day. Bud had offered too, but I hated that he was wearing himself down. He needed rest, and as much as he tried to deny it, he wasn't a spring chicken. Hell, he had more than a couple decades on me, and I was beat. Tyler could do it, in my mind; all he had to do was sit on the porch, listen and watch.

In the months we'd been together, the boys had taken a liking to me, and they'd started sleeping in my room. The cabin didn't have lots of options for them, so they slept in bed with me. It was a full-size bed, big enough for me and two small boys. But it didn't quite work out that way. George was comfy and near the center, shoving me nearly to the edge, with Darie sandwiched between us. Sometime during the night Darie decided to be acrobatic, and I woke up to his little foot in my face.

I moved the foot, slid out of bed and stretched to work out the kinks.

Bud was in the bed next to us, and when I looked over, his eyes were open. I jumped. Then he blinked.

"Christ, Bud," I said in a whisper. "You're awake."

"Whatcha think? I was dead?"

"Yes."

"Probably looked that way. Who can sleep with the ruckus and the choppers?"

"Then Faye heard them?"

"More than likely. I heard her step out before you woke." Bud sat up and stretched. "She's getting cleaned up, then making food before we leave. Tyler told her to use the green soap and not the purple. Then she said you were an asshole."

"Me?"

Bud shrugged and stood. "Yep. You. Guess she liked the purple soap. I liked the purple soap. Smelled too female for me though."

"That's the reason she can't use it." I looked down at my watch; it was just after 6 a.m. "We'll let the boys sleep a little more. I'll be back."

"Where you going?"

"Making sure everything is okay." My boots were in the kitchen area, and I grabbed a chair, pulled it out and sat down. I didn't lace my boots, just stomped into them.

I was standing up and grabbing my flannel shirt when I realized I couldn't see Tyler. I peered out the window, to the chair on the porch.

He wasn't there.

After a moment's worry, I decided he'd probably walked Faye to the shower block, since the one in the cabin didn't work. He'd be hanging out there to make sure everything was fine.

I opened the door and immediately realized that wasn't the case. Faye wasn't fine. The moment I stepped onto the porch, I heard her scream.

15. FAYE

Tyler was sitting on the porch when I slipped out to get cleaned up. When I told him what I wanted to do, he walked me to the shower block, where he asked me to stay put while he checked out the building and lit a kerosene heater.

It was a chilly morning, and I wasn't looking forward to washing with cold water. Bud had used the generator to get the pumps working, and the water in the showers was cold. Really cold. At least the little heater made the space toasty warm.

Though he was supposed to be on the cabin porch, Tyler sat on the path outside, waiting for me to finish. I washed in spurts, talking to him intermittently. We had seen the chopper as we walked to the shower building; it had made a couple of passes.

"I don't think it saw you," Tyler said.

"I hope not." I shuddered as I rubbed the cold cloth over my chest. I used the green soap, as recommended. It was strong and had a harsh, soapy smell. I'd never liked that even before the virus, but at least I would smell like everyone else. Except Darie, who was hard put to let us wash him. I think it was a fear that went back to the first day we met him, when he was coated in a layer of dead flesh and maggots. Dodge had to pull each and every maggot from his hair.

After finishing, I stayed close to the heater to keep warm as I got dressed, even putting on those ridiculous, heavy man boots Dodge insisted on.

"You never know when we're gonna have to hike it or run," he'd said. "So the flip flops are out."

Hike it or run? I could barely walk in those boots. But like with the soap, I'd do it.

I felt good, and I was ready to make some breakfast for the kids. We had powdered eggs that I'd cook up with a can of corned beef hash. Dodge would be happy, since I'd been inundating him with Spam for breakfast.

Dodge.

I'd thought a lot about him before I fell asleep, and when I woke up, I peeked in on the boys cuddling and crowding him on the bed.

Dodge was a good man. He gave me hope that people would keep their humanity even in the wake of a ravaged world.

Not wanting to cause a fire, I reached for the heater, then stopped. "Ty," I called out. "Is there a special way to shut this off? Do I just turn the knob or will the kerosene still seep?"

I didn't get a reply.

"Tyler?" I walked to the door. Had he gone back to the house? He hadn't been sitting directly by the door, but a few paces down the path. He'd heard me every other time I called out. It was strange that he would leave the "Faye is washing" post without telling me.

I opened the door and called out. "Tyler?"

Hank was standing there. The man from the highway. I jumped in surprise.

"Hey there. Faye, is it?"

I didn't have time to register if he was alone or if that other guy, Powell, was with him. Instinctively I knew this wasn't a good situation, and without hesitating I tried to shut the door.

Too slow. Too late. Hank pushed forward, grabbed my arm and yanked me out. Before I could scream, he pulled me into him and covered my mouth. My eyes watered from the stench of his fingers, pressed hard under my nose. They smelled foul.

He held me around the waist, my back pressed to his chest. I squirmed—I wasn't going to be an easy take. But I wasn't some martial arts master or a rough, tough *Mad Max* woman who could perform phenomenal feats of combat. I was just scared, and that worsened when I saw the snide look on Powell's face as he approached.

He retracted a fist; I saw it coming. With everything I had, I kicked back with my heavy boot, hoping to connect with Hank's shin.

I got him, and his grip released at the same time Powell's fist sailed forward.

In my greatest fantasy, Powell would have hit Hank, but I didn't have time to look—I just ran.

I didn't make it far. Not because they got me, but because I saw Tyler lying on the ground next to his folding chair. There was blood all around him. I screamed.

Run to the cabin, I thought. *Run. Get Dodge. Get help.*

I'd just made it to the end of the path where it reached the clearing before the cabin when I saw Dodge. I heaved out the biggest sigh of relief and focused on him charging my way.

Hank or Powell, I didn't know which one, grabbed me from behind. But that didn't stop Dodge. He was a blur in my peripheral vision. Everything moved so fast. Dodge threw a massive blow at whoever was on my left. Then he grabbed him and tossed him down.

It was Powell. And at that moment, Hank released me.

"Run," Dodge said.

Hank went for Dodge, and that was a mistake. He was enraged, and they were no match for him.

"Run," Dodge hollered again, now fighting both men.

Run where? My first instinct was to go to Tyler. As I turned, I saw two more men approaching from behind Dodge. Before I could yell out a warning, one of them raised a bat and swept it down toward Dodge as if he were going for a grand slam.

It struck Dodge against the upper back, and as he teetered forward, the man slammed the bat down again, hitting Dodge in the head.

Blood sprayed out and Dodge went down.

I thought they'd killed him.

A screamed of fear and worry, a cry for help, rumbled from my belly through my chest.

Dodge was down.

The four men pounced on him, viciously kicking him, striking him. I didn't know what to do, how to help. My heart was racing out of control. Dodge was beaten and Tyler was hurt, or worse.

Tyler. Tyler had a gun.

I spun to race the few feet to the boy and skidded to a stop at the first echoing boom of a shotgun.

I glanced over my shoulder to see Powell flying up and backwards through the air. A second shot was fired, and baseball bat man went down.

Bud was on the porch of the cabin. He engaged the chamber again, shifted his body and blasted the third man. He stood there for a moment, waiting, and when Hank stumbled to his feet, he shot him as well.

Both of the Cash men were down for the count. "Help him," I yelled to Bud as I turned. "Tyler's hurt."

I ran as fast as I could to poor Tyler. The young man looked so helpless, lying on the ground on his side. There was a pool of blood around his stomach.

My hands shook as I reached for his shoulder, and he groaned. I sighed. He was alive.

He hadn't been shot; it looked as if he'd been knifed in the gut. Gently, I rolled him onto his back and removed my sweatshirt. He was bleeding badly and I didn't know what to do. Cover the wound was all I knew, cover and pressure.

I placed my bunched-up sweatshirt over the huge gash in his gut.

"Faye," he said weakly. "I'm sorry."

"No, sweetie. No. It's gonna be fine." I felt the emotions creep up my throat. His face was pale, and I applied more pressure.

I was panicking. I couldn't breathe. I wanted to scream and cry out. This wasn't happening. It wasn't. I looked around, left to right, wanting help. But this wasn't the old world. There wasn't anyone to call, to come rushing to the aid of a fallen teenager.

Or was there?

I was at the edge of insanity, ready to lose it, when he came running down the path. It was a soldier, or at least he was dressed like one. He wore camouflage pants, a dirty green T-shirt and a military jacket that hung open. He slid in on his knees like a baseball player, dropping a backpack next to Tyler.

"Let me look." He removed my trembling hands from the sweatshirt and lifted it slightly. "Farmer!" he called out. "Hold this," he said to me.

I did. Who was this man?

"Farmer!" he called out again. "Stat. One down."

A younger man, thin and also in uniform, ran down the path toward us. He had a bigger pack, which he set down by Tyler's head.

"I got this, Major."

The "major" acknowledged with a nod, and stood. "I'll go assist Lane with the other man."

I looked briefly at him as he walked away, then back to Farmer, who was reaching into his bag.

"I'm Lieutenant Farmer. I'm a flight medic. What is his name?" he asked as he pulled out a syringe.

"Tyler," I said.

"Tyler," Farmer said. "Hey, Tyler, look at me. Open your eyes. Let me know you're with us."

Tyler opened his eyes.

"Good. Good boy. You're gonna be okay," Farmer said. "I'm gonna give you something right now for the pain. It will relax you, so I can help. And another injection of antibiotics. Don't need you getting sick."

Farmer worked quickly, injecting the medication then scooting down more toward the wound. He flipped open the backpack, which was filled with different items. I didn't know what they all were, though some looked like bandages.

After ripping open a huge gauze pad, Farmer removed the sweatshirt. "Looks like a hunting knife." He probed the wound with his fingers, his face scrunching up. "Deep, too. Hold this on here," he said to me, then reached back into his bag.

I was holding the pad when the major returned. He was of average height and build, nothing extraordinary, but he projected strength, though wasn't at all overbearing. I couldn't tell his age, but his face was worn and his brown hair was dashed with some gray. All of which could have occurred after the virus. He looked forty but could have been thirty.

"How is he?" the major asked.

Farmer exhaled and shook his head. "I don't know. Whatever they gutted him with hit something. We have internal bleeding. What about the man?"

"Alive. Strong guy. Lane said a couple broken ribs, arm is broken. Head injury. He doesn't think it's a fractured skull or that he has any internal bleeding. He wants you to assess. But nothing a few days' rest won't help with. What about him?"

"We do nothing and the kid bleeds out. I can perform field surgery but … that's not the best option. Major, he weighs no more than a buck fifty."

The major looked at me. "Is this your son?"

I answered quickly. "Yes."

"Then he goes too. Stabilize him." The major turned away.

He goes? My mind raced, and I was about to ask what that meant when another solider approached the major.

"What do you want me to do?" the soldier asked.

"Radio Carlisle base. Tell them we're flying in with the mission and an injured male. The rest of the squad can drive there. We'll take first transport down. Administer what is needed for the injured man, and get the men to clear out those bodies. There are kids, for crying out loud. Make sure the old man is fine, and needs nothing. Map out the route and leave the kids some candy." The major walked off down the path.

"Ma'am," Farmer called.

I looked at him. He held what looked like a huge syringe, but there wasn't a needle. It wasn't clear, but blue, and it was wide. "What is that?"

"It's injectable field foam. It will coat the insides and stop the bleeding until we can get him into surgery. We use it in combat. Just need you to hold him still, 'cause I have to go into the wound and inject."

I nodded, intent on following his instructions. "You'll go check on Dodge after this?"

"The other injured man?" he asked as he worked. "Yes. But Lane is pretty good."

"Who are you people?"

"United States Army. I am, at least. Lane is Air Force. But what does that matter now, right?"

"What are you doing here?"

"We were looking for you. Been following you since Pennsylvania."

"Why?"

"You're kidding, right?" He smiled briefly. "You're the last woman. And good thing for you guys we arrived when we did."

Everything seemed like a dream, a bad dream. One moment happy family, the next devastated by reality. All I could do was hope for the best and pray it all worked out.

I stayed with Tyler until Farmer said he was stable. They'd be moving him soon, and me for that matter—they instructed me to get my things. I wasn't given a choice. But I had questions, and I knew the major could answer them.

As soon as I emerged into the clearing by the cabin, the major in my sights, George ran to me and hugged me.

"I'm okay," I said.

"I was worried. How's Ty?"

"Bad. Where's Dodge?" I didn't see him, or the bodies.

"Inside. They are fixing his arm. He's not awake."

The major must have heard this, because he walked over. "He'll be out for a day or so, but we believe he'll be fine. We'll give you a few moments to get your things."

"Wait. Wait." I held up my hands.

"Are we leaving?" George asked innocently.

The major answered. "Son, she's coming with us. We gave the older man directions to where we're going."

"Where am I going?" I asked. "I can't leave my family."

"You have an obligation to your country," he said. "An obligation to the human race to go."

"I'm not going to be a human guinea pig."

"I give you my word that is not the case. Yes, there will be tests, but it needs to be done."

"I'm not going. You can't make me go," I said adamantly.

"You are absolutely right. My orders are to get you no matter what. Willing or not. But if you tell me you are not going, then I am reporting that I lost you. I don't agree with taking you against your will. Understand?"

"I understand."

"Then understand this. Your son is seriously injured. He needs help that we can provide. Without it, when that foam disintegrates, he'll bleed out. Flying him to our survivor camp is his best hope. He goes with you or he doesn't go at all."

"That's blackmail," I said.

"Yeah, well, how about this for blackmail. Your family was in danger because of you being a woman. *You* were in danger. Do you think if the old man hadn't fired, those men would have left the little ones alone? No. For their protection and yours, this is the best thing."

I pursed my lips. I could feel a lump in my stomach, especially when George whined out a "No."

I turned to him and crouched down. "I don't want to go, or leave you. But Tyler needs me to help him."

"I need you, Faye. Don't you need us, too?"

"Oh my God, with all my heart." I grabbed him and embraced him. "But when big tough Dodge wakes up, he's gonna need you, because he's going to be sad. So you keep him strong and get him to me." I pulled back, then cupped his face in my hands. "Okay?"

He pouted as he nodded.

I put my lips to his cheek. "Be strong. I will be thinking of you and waiting for you."

His head hung and it broke my heart. I hated leaving him and Darie, and I wouldn't have gone with the soldiers if Tyler hadn't needed the help. They could help him, from what I'd witnessed, and the way they worked on him right then and there told me they weren't bad men; they were doing their job, and that was to get me. While it appeared as if I were leaving without thought, that wasn't the case. I was going for Tyler—Dodge would want that. Refusing to go would endanger Dodge's son. After all we had been through, I would not nor could not let Dodge lose another child.

As I walked by the major, he stopped me. "I don't mean to be a hard ass. For you and them, this really needs to be done."

I acknowledged him with a nod and went to the cabin. George stayed close behind me. As soon as I stepped inside, I thought how great it would be to be a four-year-old like Darie. If he'd been fazed by everything that was happening, he had already moved on and was sitting at the table playing with a truck.

Bud was talking to another soldier, and he made eye contact with me. I pointed to the back bedroom before going through. I heard the soldier speaking as I gathered my things. He was explaining the medication he was leaving and what Bud was to do, and apparently he had given Bud a speed course on changing IVs, because he mentioned leaving a replacement bag.

I didn't take much, some pictures and half my clothes. I did, however, take the Wilkes watch that I'd had since waking up in that stadium. I always had it with me; it had been with me from the very beginning of my journey.

I also took the small truck that Darie had made me, and the items I'd brought that had belonged to my own children. I stuffed my purple soap in the bag, because it didn't matter anymore if I smelled feminine.

I'd been found.

I shouldered the bag and stepped out of the room. Farmer was examining Dodge, and that was the first time I got a good look at him.

An ache filled my entire chest. Dodge was strong, yet looked so hurt and helpless on that sofa. He had his head bandaged, an arm in an air cast, chest wrapped, an IV in, and his eyes closed.

Darie was consumed with his toy, and I made my goodbye to him quick and without drama. I didn't want to stir fear in the child. I kissed him, hugged him and said I would see him soon.

I stood by Bud, waiting for Farmer to finish. Bud rubbed a hand up and down my back. "You all right?" he asked.

Arms folded close to my body, I nodded. "Poor Dodge."

"He took a hell of a beating."

"Thank you." I turned to Bud. "Thank you for shooting—"

He stopped me with a shake of his head. "Didn't do nothing no one else wouldn't do. How's the boy?"

"He's bad. That's the only reason I'm leaving."

"I know. And they gave us directions, so we'll be there. Might be a while. God knows how long it will take, and we aren't leaving till he's well. But we'll get there. I promise."

I reached out to Bud and embraced him. "Watch them."

"And you take care of Tyler and yourself."

"I'm scared."

"Me too."

He kissed me on the cheek and I closed my eyes.

Farmer cleared his throat, and I looked at him. "How is he?" I asked.

"Everything that Lane said is spot on. He'll be fine in a week, but he shouldn't move for a few days. He'll probably wake up tomorrow, but he's got a head injury." Farmer looked at Bud. "Don't be surprised if he's a little out of it for a couple days."

"My wife had a head injury once," Bud said. "I remember."

"Good. Ma'am, we gotta go. We need to get to the chopper."

"I understand. I just need a minute."

Farmer shook hands with Bud, wished him luck then slipped out.

I had said my goodbyes to Darie, George and Bud, and I just needed to say goodbye to Dodge. I didn't realize how hard it was going to be until I stepped toward the couch.

"Dodge," I whispered as I knelt by him. "I know you can't hear me. Maybe you can." I grabbed his hand. "Thank you for coming to my rescue. I promise with everything I am to watch your son. He means the world to me, too. All of you do. Get well." I leaned closer, my mouth near his ear. "Get strong, then come and get me." I kissed his forehead softly, leaving my lips to linger there before I finally stood.

Every bit of my insides shook. I was scared to death. They had become a part of me, George, Darie, Bud, Tyler and Dodge. Leaving them was like leaving a security blanket. I didn't want to walk away. I gathered what little courage I had and left, holding on to the hope that it wasn't the last time I'd see them, and that before long we'd be reunited.

16. MAJOR JAMES REYNOLDS

The RV was our tip off. We knew Dodge was traveling in one with an old man and two boys, and that a woman named Faye had called out to him. When we spotted the RV on a highway in Ohio we had a good inkling it was them. Farmer was flying the chopper and reported that they had stopped at a campsite.

I arrived there before dawn. I didn't even see the marauders enter the camp.

But at least we were able to save the young man. He wasn't out of the woods, but he stood a better chance with us. The north-east regional squads were directed to head back down to COM Camp. The other squads scattered about the country were still on a directive to find other women. Giving up on that search meant giving up on the race. We'd keep searching until we exhausted our resources.

This woman, Faye, could not carry that burden alone.

Physically she was fine; emotionally she wasn't. She sat with me and Tyler in the back of the truck and watched like a lost puppy as we pulled away from the camp. I could see it on her face, the sadness, as the little boy ran after us until we had gone too far. She sobbed when he disappeared from sight.

The chopper was waiting on the highway and we lifted safely. Tyler's vitals were holding strong, but we had to move fast. We were six hours from the foam breaking down. I was hopeful the plane would be ready when we reached Carlisle.

Even as we lifted, Faye kept staring out the window. She admitted to me that Tyler wasn't actually her son, and I told her that, like a priest, I would keep her confession confidential.

It was for the best if everyone at camp believed he was her child. Not that I doubted the care he'd get, but it was an assurance they'd give their all.

She didn't speak after that; the noise from the chopper was too loud. In fact, she didn't say a word until we were on the plane and airborne. She stayed next to Tyler.

I offered her water and a breakfast biscuit. She took both, and after she thanked me, she asked me my name.

"Reynolds. Major Reynolds."

"What is your first name?"

"I'm sorry." I sat down on the bench across from her. "It's James."

"Where are we going?"

"COM Camp," I replied. "There are five division bases in the Panhandle of Florida. The main complex is located north-west of the Apalachicola National Forest."

"COM Camp?"

"Acronym. Continuity of Mankind. The primary base, the medical research center and housing were developed many years ago. It's like an outdoor biosphere, best way I can describe it. No one thought it would ever be used."

"When did they start moving people there?"

"When they had a viable cure and treatment."

She immediately locked eyes with me. "If they can cure it, why is it a dead world?"

"They cured it too late. So now they are moving on to the next phase. Continuity of Mankind. We can go back to the old way of life, but that plan ends if we don't find a solution."

"I'm not the only one."

"Let's hope."

"What are they going to do to me?" she asked.

"Medically, I don't know. Like I said, there will be tests."

"Will I be a prisoner?"

"You'll be protected."

"A prisoner."

"Ma'am ..."

"Faye."

"Faye ... You have to be protected. Right now it's still early, people are still healing. But a couple more months, no women, it's not going to be good. You need to be secured."

"A prisoner."

"No." I shook my head. "Not at all."

"Will I get to be with Tyler?"

"I don't see why not."

"You aren't bringing me down there to be part of some sick sexual lottery, are you?"

As wrong as it was, as inappropriate as it seemed, I laughed. I quickly cleared my throat. "No."

She made a non-committal grunt and turned her head.

"This entire thing is a scary prospect, I understand that. You won't be a prisoner, mistreated or a lottery prize. I give you my word. I know you don't know me and have no reason to trust me. But my word is all I have left in this godforsaken world, and that isn't going to hell too."

She turned back and stared at me. I think she accepted my promise.

She was scared, rightfully so. One moment she's moving on with a group she trusts, trying to put her life back together, and the next she's swept away, taken as a means to save the human race.

Was that even possible? That was still to be determined.

Her fears were founded. There *was* uncertainty there. I didn't know what they had planned for Faye, but I would do all I could to make sure it wasn't the nightmare she was fearing. Because before we could even begin to save the human race, we had to first preserve our humanity.

17. FAYE

It was the first time I had been in a helicopter, and thankfully I was more worried about Tyler than I was about the flight. His body shook and jolted with every sway of the bird. He remained unconscious the entire time. Farmer told me it was the medication he'd given him and that resting was for the best.

We arrived at an Army base somewhere mid-Pennsylvania. A small military cargo plane was waiting, and as soon as we boarded we took off faster than I would have believed possible. Farmer kept checking on Tyler, telling me he was doing well. But I could see his belly starting to distend. I asked about it; I wasn't a doctor, but even to me it didn't look right.

It was the internal bleeding, and the clock was ticking between the disintegrating foam and the desperate need for surgery.

The flight took two hours, and a van was waiting when we arrived. There were no windows in the back of it, and all I knew was it was hot. Muggy and hot.

The major—James—didn't really speak unless I spoke to him first. He sat across from me on the plane and behind me in the back of the van. He gave promise after promise that I wasn't going to be some test subject hooked up to machines. I envisioned my prison camp as a hospital room. I'd wear nothing but a hospital gown and be kept in a white room with white walls. No one would find me, and I'd watch life, or what I could of it, through a lab window.

That was what I believed. What else could there be?

We stopped only once, and from what I could hear being said, it was a checkpoint. We continued on for only a short distance before the van braked to a halt and the back doors were flung open.

We were greeted by two men in hospital scrubs, standing with a gurney. They immediately grabbed Tyler. As I hurried from the van to be with him, I was met by a man in his late thirties, clean cut, looking every bit the doctor, right down to the tie around his neck.

Was I in a twilight zone? Who wore a tie in a dystopian world?

I looked to my left. We were at a small hospital; at least, it looked that way.

Tie-wearing hospital guy placed his hands on my shoulders and smiled broadly. "We are so happy to have you. We'll take good care of him."

"I want to go with him."

"Absolutely." He pointed to the building. "This way."

He led the way inside. It was without a doubt a hospital. We walked through an emergency area, and though it didn't buzz like the hospitals of pre-virus days, there were people there waiting to be seen. Some of them were children cradling injured limbs. It was a picture of normality … just on a very small scale.

They were all male.

Everyone stopped what they were doing to look at me.

At the end of a series of short halls, they took Tyler through a set of double doors. A man approached me. "He's going into surgery now, and Dr. Lewis and I can wait to talk to you. We have a very good surgeon here."

"Who are you?" I asked.

"Barry Chatham. I'm a geneticist, and I've been working on the virus. I'll be working closely with you. Would you like to go to your new home and wait on news of your son there?"

"I'd like to wait here."

"Very well. Can I get you something? Coffee? Tea?"

Did he just ask if I wanted coffee? "Coffee, thanks," I stuttered.

He nodded and turned away. James was standing behind him. "Major, make sure there is a guard on this door or in there."

"Yes, sir," James replied. "I'm assigned for now, and then I'm heading back home to clean up. I've been out there a while."

"I'm not running away," I said.

James looked at me. "Faye, it's really for your protection. We think you're safe, but you never know."

Chatham opened a door and gestured for me to go through. He closed it and left me alone. The room was small; there were two chairs, a couch, a coffee table and a television with an old video player that was showing old *I Love Lucy* reruns.

Chatham returned only once, and that was to bring me the promised coffee and a blanket in case I got chilled. I was, oddly enough; the room was air-conditioned.

A handful of episodes of *I Love Lucy* later, they brought me some soup. Night had fallen by the time I heard anything about Tyler.

A man came into the room and introduced himself as Dr. Drescoll. My heart dropped to my stomach as I waited to hear what he had to say.

"He's good and stable. We repaired all the damage."

I exhaled loudly. "Can I see him?"

"Yes. But we are keeping him in a medically induced coma, just to allow his body to rest. He lost a lot of blood, and it appears when they inserted the knife, they ripped upward. He's a lucky young man. With rest, he'll make it."

He took me to see Tyler, who was indeed sleeping. He was hooked up with intravenous lines, and a heart monitor beeped steadily.

Barry Chatham returned and asked if I was ready to go get some rest. Though I hated to leave Tyler, I said yes. When he escorted me down the hall, I figured it was now that they'd take me, strip me, scrub me down like an infected person and start draining my blood.

To say I was relieved to see James was an understatement. I actually barely recognized him at first, because he was clean.

"Major Reynolds will walk with us," Barry said.

I was fine with that. He, Farmer and Lane were the only ones I knew. I was surprised when James took my pack.

We went out of the hospital, and though it was dark, I got my first look around. The weather was still warm and muggy. The street was flat and narrow. Two-lane roads. It looked like a cross between a military base and a small town.

We walked two blocks and stopped when we reached a five-story apartment-type building set back on a larger section of property. A long, tall fence with barbed wire surrounded the entire area around it. There were armed guards positioned out front, and they unlocked the gate to let us in.

"My prison?" I asked James.

"If it is, it's my prison too. I live in this building. I'm still getting used to the fence."

"It's new," Barry said. "We erected it when we started our search for you. All it takes is one person to want to get to you. This is the safest building I can think of. About twenty of our military personnel reside here."

The building reminded me more of a motel. Outside stairwells, hallways that ran the length of each floor. A single metal door for each unit and a window next to it.

There was a small lobby and a single elevator. We took it to the fifth floor and walked the exterior hallway all the way to the very end. A soldier was sitting in a chair by the door; he stood when we approached.

"I'll leave you to get situated," Barry said. "Major Reynolds will see you in. He's made sure the place is ready for you. There should be plenty of food and water, and please do not leave without an escort—please."

"I understand," I replied.

"I expect you'll go to the hospital in the morning to see Tyler. I would like to take time to talk to you with Dr. Lewis about the tests we'd like to run on you."

"What kind of tests?"

"Blood. We'll do lots of blood tests. We need to find out why you survived and other females did not. Most of this is to preserve and to protect the only woman we know that has survived. And possibly, you know, getting you to part with some ova. But we'll discuss that tomorrow. For now, get some rest." He gave my shoulder a squeeze and stepped back, turned, walked a couple feet and stopped. "And Faye, thank you for joining us."

I wanted to say, "Did I have a choice?" But my mind was still spinning over the fact that he had so nonchalantly asked for my eggs.

"This way." James turned the knob and pushed open the door. "It's not much." He flicked on the light. "But it's clean, air-conditioned, and has hot water."

I kept thinking, *Not much?* It had power, lights and a stove. If there was hot water, more than likely there was a toilet. I had been living for months cooking on a fire or a Coleman stove, using lanterns and candles, going to the bathroom in a makeshift outhouse. And I'd thought that was pretty darned good living in a world that had gone to pot.

The apartment unit was simple and plain. We stepped into a living room that also served as a dining area with a small two-seat table. The kitchen was open plan except for a counter that served as a small partition.

"Hall is that way." James pointed. "To the bedroom and bathroom. There is food. And …" He walked over to the kitchen counter. "I hope you don't mind—I took the liberty of getting you this."

He held up a bottle of bourbon. "Want one?"

"Yes, thank you."

He cracked open the bottle, reached for a short glass and poured.

"What made you believe I drink?" I asked.

He handed me the glass. "I found where you were staying before you went to Ohio. My God, the empty bottles."

"Yeah, that was a means of pain relief long before the virus."

"I hear you on that one." He stepped back, letting out a deep breath. "Anyhow, if you need anything, just let the guard know. I'm also right next door."

"Thank you."

"Not a problem." He walked to the door. "Good night, Faye."

I lifted my glass. "Night, James."

He stepped out.

Admittedly, when that door closed, I felt a jolt of nerves. The apartment, COM Camp … even Dr. Chatham wasn't at all what I'd expected. Everything was too nice, too easy, and that in turn made me leery.

I sat down on the couch, intent on sipping my drink. It had been a long, stressful and agonizing day. I thought of the boys and hoped they were okay. I missed them—I missed them terribly. The next morning would be quiet without their mad laughter and shenanigans. I thought and prayed for Dodge to get well and come get me. I thought of Tyler and how lucky he was to be alive.

I took another sip and sat back in the couch. I wouldn't overthink my circumstances, not on the first night. But I would the next day. It seemed too good to be true, and in the world we lived in, that was something I just couldn't allow myself to trust.

18. DODGE

Upon first awakening—at least, I thought it was the first—my last recollection was pulling into the campground. I had lost everything after that moment. I didn't know why I had some tube in my arm, why my head pounded worse than any hangover and why I couldn't move an inch without excruciating pain radiating up my side.

It was dark. Bud slept in a chair near me, an old newspaper spread across his lap.

He looked dead. Before I could call out, or even register what was going on, I passed out again.

The sound of the boys laughing and running summoned me to, and I jolted awake with what felt like a great crash of thunder.

My mistake was jerking up to a sitting position. I screamed out in pain, which of course scared the hell out of Darie, and he screamed as well.

"Dodge is a zombie! Dodge is a zombie!" His voice trailed off as he ran away.

"Dodge ain't no zombie." Bud walked into sight. "Dumb move, sitting up like that. Do you know my name?"

"It's Bud," I said with some sarcasm.

"Know who the president was?"

"Keene."

"Where are you?'

"Ohio, some campsite."

"Good. Good." Bud winked.

"Dodge!" George flew into the room, stopping just as he reached for me. "You're okay?"

"Yeah."

"What's my name?"

"George."

"Dodge, you're normal." He hugged me. Even his frail arms hurt my body, but that was okay.

Bud walked over, removed George then placed pillows behind my back so I could sit up comfortably.

"Need some water?" Bud asked. "Anything?"

"Water and an aspirin."

"We have better stuff for ya."

I didn't understand that, and I guess my facial expression conveyed as much.

"What's the last you remember?" Bud asked.

I paused to think. At first, again, when I'd opened my eyes the night before, I could only recall pulling into the campsite. Everything was a fog, hard to remember at all.

"Think. Do you remember those two men on the highway?"

"Yeah, I—" Suddenly a vision of Hank holding Faye flashed into my mind. I blinked, then I saw Powell. I was engulfed with rage. I remembered swinging, throwing one of them, fighting and then … nothing. "Oh my God, Faye." Again, I tried to get up. The pain was too much, and Bud stopped me.

He told George to take Darie into the back and play a game. George obliged, and Bud sat on the coffee table, hands folded.

"Tell me she's okay," I said.

"Faye is fine. Thanks to you. Unfortunately you were jumped by two more men. They hit you pretty hard then clobbered you with a bat. Two busted ribs, your arm is broke and you have a pretty bad head injury. Your whole body has to be aching."

"How did it end?"

"I shot them. But Faye is fine, unscathed. Tyler, on the other hand, not so much."

"Oh my God, my son."

"He's not dead." Bud held up his hands. "They gutted him pretty good with a knife."

"Where is he?"

"Not here. With Faye."

At that point I was swimming in confusion. "Where are they?"

"Army came and took them. Faye went because they needed to get Tyler help. He was pretty bad. They flew them out."

I felt an ache in my chest, totally defeated. I'd failed.

"It had to be done," Bud said. "They weren't meaning Faye any harm, and when you're well, we'll head down there. They gave me directions."

"How do you know? How do you know they didn't mean her harm or they weren't just gonna kill my kid?"

"'Cause in my years on this earth, Dodge, I've become a pretty good judge of character. That major that headed the team? Good fella. Two young medics that worked on you and Tyler. All good intentions. If they hadn't arrived when they did, Tyler would have died."

"When did they leave?"

"Two days ago."

"Two days? I've been out two days?"

"Not really," Bud replied. "You got up a few times."

"I don't remember."

"I figured you wouldn't. You were out of it, talking crazy stuff. One time when I asked you what my name was, you said it was Clint Eastwood. At first I thought you were joking, because I shot those men, but then you said you were in Kentucky the day after prom and the president was Reagan. Those two time frames don't even match up."

I brought my hand to my head. It was throbbing.

"The Army left pain medication if you want it."

"Yeah. Maybe. I just want to get up and go."

"Well, you aren't doing that. Not today, at least. When I know you are getting better and thinking clearly, and can move with less pain, then we'll hit the road."

"I'm thinking clearly," I said.

"Right now. My wife fractured her skull when she was sixty-five, trying to ride one of those electric scooters. Wasn't right in the head for two weeks. Some days she was lucid, others she was playing bingo with the cereal box. Let's just be sure; I don't need to be chasing aliens when we're on the road."

"Aliens?"

"Yeah, that was one story you gave."

I breathed out heavily and sat back. "I feel like I failed her. How did I let this happen?"

"You didn't let this happen. You did all that you could. None of us thought our camp would be attacked. By God's grace we're all alive. You get well and strong and we hit the road. Those boys need you and so does Faye." Bud stood. "I'll go get that pain medication and you rest up. I'll tell George not to read to you."

"Why would you do that? He's allowed to read to me. I love that."

"I know you do, but not now. Please. Every time he read you a story, you opened your eyes and believed you lived that reality. Although that could be funny if he read *Brokeback Mountain* to you."

Bud chuckled at his own joke as he walked away. I just groaned again, rested back and closed my eyes. Despite what Bud had said, I still felt heavily defeated. Defeated and in pain. I would do my best to get my strength up enough to leave. I didn't want to waste any more time getting to my son and Faye.

Bud may have trusted those men, but me, I didn't. I feared the worst in what they could possibly do to Tyler, and even worse, to Faye.

19. FAYE

Tyler took a turn for the worse that first morning, exactly twenty-four hours after the attack. He developed a fever and his belly began to swell again. I woke up having slept on the couch; the hot shower I took the night before had plummeted me into a wall of exhaustion. I didn't sleep long, and knew the second I opened my eyes that something was wrong.

I dressed and told the soldier outside my door I wanted to go to the hospital to see Tyler. He walked me to the hospital and notified James I was there. I didn't see him at all that morning. For some reason I was under the impression he was my personal guard. But that wasn't the case. He was a busy man; I was one mission accomplished, and one of the soldiers told me he was prepping teams to go out following rumors of more surviving women. They were only rumors; no one had really seen one.

I was the only woman they knew for sure existed.

Tyler was still sleeping when I arrived, but I noticed his color was off, even more so than the day before. A doctor came in and told me Tyler had an infection. He explained that the knife had probably been full of bacteria. They loaded him with antibiotics, but by late afternoon they had to go back in and not only find the "bleeder," but clear out some of the infection.

There was a tube extending out of Tyler's abdomen, and the need for a medically induced coma was increasing. I didn't leave his side. Dodge wouldn't want his son alone, and I didn't want him to be alone either.

By the following morning his fever had dropped, and by dinner time he was declared out of the woods and I was instructed to go get some rest. What surprised me was the fact that I still hadn't met Dr. Lewis. Barry Chatham had stopped in, merely to check on Tyler and me. He told me his concern was for me to be in a controlled and protected environment and that when things calmed down he would speak to me about what they needed.

I accepted that and decided to go back to my apartment. They promised they would get me if needed.

No one really spoke to me; I just stayed in that room. When I did walk outside, it seemed as if all activity stopped. The men and boys just stared at me.

Despite my new surroundings I still expected to see Dodge at any moment. Farmer told me he was probably just coming to up north, and since he was traveling with Bud and the boys, to give them a good week to get to me, maybe even ten days.

They were on my mind constantly. It was almost exactly four months since I'd met Dodge, and I'd spent almost every single day with him and the boys, along with Bud. Now I was pushing the third night without them, and I was lost. I missed my nighttime hugs from Darie. He'd curl up on my lap until he was just about to go to sleep, and then after catching himself, he'd race to Dodge to put him to bed. I missed listening to George reading to Dodge with impressive skill. He did that every night; whatever he could find, he'd read. Dodge would listen and comment, and George would even quiz him to make sure he was paying attention. Dodge always did.

Life at my house with them and Bud was like a prepping-meets-camping trip. It was easy, relaxed, and even though we'd led a colonial-style life, it had a sense of normalcy.

Even with my air-conditioning, hot water and modern conveniences, which were lost for ninety-nine percent of the world, I wanted to go back to the simplicity and to the people that had become no less than a family to me.

After a shower, I ate some sort of stew from a can, grabbed the bottle and glass and decided it was such a warm night I'd sit out; the room had patio doors at the back leading onto a balcony. There were two chairs, the lounge kind, and a table between them. I lit a candle and enjoyed my drink.

It gave me a sense of comfort because it was part of my nightly routine. Every night, no matter what, after the boys were down Dodge and I sat on my deck. It was our thing. There was only one night that we hadn't done so, and that was when Darie had caught a stomach bug. Dodge and I had taken turns with Darie as he hovered over a bucket.

It was hard to believe that seven months had passed since my family had died. I had wanted to die. Never would I have believed that it would take a dead world to bring me back to life.

Not a day went by that I didn't think of my husband, my daughter and son. But no longer did I think of them with an abundance of sadness; I'd started to reach the point where I remembered the fun times. The happiness they'd given me.

In the midst of my thoughts, I heard a door slide open; I shared the balcony with the apartment next to mine. Only a railing separated us.

I glanced over to see James; he held a glass and bottle as he stepped out.

He looked surprised to see me. "I'm sorry," he said. "If you want privacy out here, I can go back in."

"No, please. That's fine. Enjoy your drink."

He nodded and sat down on a chair. "I hear Tyler is doing better."

"Yes, they expect to see him really improve over the next couple days."

"How are you doing?"

I shrugged. "Worried about Tyler, can't stop thinking about Darie and George. Bud, too. And Dodge, I am so worried about him."

"He's a tough guy," James said. "He'll be fine. I have a feeling."

"Thank you for that. I haven't seen you in a couple days. One of your soldier guys was telling me you were getting search parties ready. Are you going back out?"

James shook his head. "Not this time. I promised you that you would be fine. I don't want to be too far away."

"I appreciate that. So I take it you weren't too far away these past couple days?"

"Fifteen miles. Division Five camp. We had some issues."

"What kind?" I asked, then waved my hand. "I'm sorry, none of my business."

"No, that's fine. Just a bit of trouble. Division Five camp houses our rough survivors."

"You have them all together in one camp? Is that smart? I mean, putting all the bad together is like a prison. You can only breed more bad."

"I agree. But it's not my call. I am only following orders."

"From who?"

"Excuse me?"

"Who gives the orders? Chatham? Lewis?"

"In anything medical they do. About you they do, sort of, but they aren't in charge of COM Camp."

"Who is?"

"The president and a skeleton staff."

That took me by surprise. "The president is alive? How did he survive the virus?"

"He's the president. First sign of problems, they locked him in an airtight room. Then the vaccine was found and he was one of the first to get it. But his family got sick right away—you know that, though."

"Nope." I shook my head. "I caught the beginning of the outbreak, but I missed the grand finale." I downed the rest of my drink and refilled my glass. I looked at it as I spoke. "All those bottles you found at my house kind of contributed to it. I was in an alcoholic coma when the world went to shit. Drank myself into oblivion. I didn't want to feel; I wanted to be numb."

"I'm sorry. Was it the outbreak? You said you caught the beginning of it. Did you lose family?"

"Not to the virus. I … Three months before everyone died, everyone I loved was killed in a car accident." Instinctively drawn by that flash of memory, I downed my drink. I looked over as James huffed; it sounded almost like laughter. I was insulted. "Was that funny?"

"Nope." He took a big gulp and gasped. "Familiar." With a grunt, he reached for his own bottle. "Five months before everything ended, I had just finished my last day on my tour overseas. I was on my way back and the plan was to meet my family on vacation. Unfortunately, their plane had trouble. Flight 247 outside of Orlando—it crashed."

I gasped. "Oh my God, I am so sorry. I remember that crash."

"Me too. I lost my wife, my three kids, my mother, sister and niece. Everyone. Gone."

"James, I … I am so sorry. I know how you feel."

"Yeah, you do. Anyhow, like you"—he lifted his glass—"I drank a lot. Then the virus started and I went on detail. Threw myself into my work. Worked exodus checkpoints, then aid stations until I got sick."

"You got the virus too?" I said. "I caught the virus. Our stories are so similar—please don't tell me you woke up in a pile of bodies."

He looked at me sharply. "Did you?"

"Yeah, in a football stadium. I woke to a dead world. I thought I was the last woman on earth."

"You are."

"So far," I said. "But I also thought I was the only living person."

"I had the same thoughts. I woke up in an Army tent outside a body depository. Everyone dead. No one around. And while I'd suffered with the illness, I thought my suffering was over."

I shifted in my chair to face him. "How did you do it? How did you not want to die? I woke up and spent every second of my life wanting to die. What got you past that point?"

"Not sure that I am."

"You still want to die?"

"I don't know." He gave a half-shrug. "I'm not sure if I want to die, I just haven't had anything that made me want to go on. You know? I may have survived, but unfortunately ..." He paused. "I still don't feel alive."

20. DODGE

The first time I really moved wasn't easy, but I was tired of pissing in a cup. My balance was a bit off, and I should have waited for some help, but I wanted to get strong. To me, lying around wasn't doing that. My body hurt with every step; I could only imagine how badly it would hurt without those pills.

I needed some air. I felt such a sense of emptiness. My son and Faye were gone. Out there in the world somewhere. I was worried sick about them, and that wouldn't help me get back to sleep. Then again, I had slept for a couple days.

It was a cooler night; I probably should have had a jacket, but I wasn't sure how I'd put it on. Any real twist of my body was agonizing. I'd been sitting on the front porch for about ten minutes when I heard the squeak of the screen door, followed by a deep sigh.

His breathing announced his presence, and then George sat down next to me.

"Hey, buddy," I said. "Can't sleep?"

"I tried. I heard you making noise and grunting."

"Sorry."

"That's okay. What are you doing? Just staring out?"

"Yep."

"Can I sit out here with you?"

"Absolutely. I'd like that."

George was breathing deeply, in and out. Almost restlessly. "I missed reading to you tonight."

"You should have."

"Bud said I'm not allowed until I find some story called *Brokeback* ... something."

"Don't listen to Bud. You can read me anything."

"Cool." Another deep breath, in, out. "You aren't looking for the giant squirrels, are you?"

I glanced at him. "What are you talking about?"

"When you woke up the one time you were yelling about giant squirrels. We had to pretend to kill them to shut you up."

"Oh my God." I ran my hand over my head.

"That's okay, you got hit on the head pretty bad."

"I figured."

"With a bat," George said.

"Better than a crowbar."

"I saved it so you can see. It still has your blood on it."

I cocked an eyebrow and looked at him. "You saved it?"

"Yeah, it's pretty cool. I'll show you."

"Tomorrow. Okay?"

"Okay." He shrugged. "Are you sitting here worried about Tyler and Faye?"

"Yeah, I am."

"They're okay, you know," George said. "The Army guys were nice. They wanted to help. Say, Dodge, you don't think they'll be so nice to her that she won't want to come back, do you?"

I didn't even need to think about that question. "Nah, she likes you guys too much."

"She likes you too, Dodge. Even though she yells at us guys. Probably because she doesn't like boys. I miss her. I miss Tyler. Do you miss them?"

"Yeah. Yeah, I do. Very much."

"You're gonna get better and get them, right? You're gonna go down there and get back Faye and Ty. Right, Dodge? 'Cause you can't fight any more bad guys if you're hurt."

"I'll get better and then we'll go. If it's the last thing I do, I'll get them and we'll be together again." I reached over, grabbed his little hand and gave it a reassuring squeeze. "I promise."

I intended to keep my promise. I would get better and we'd head down to Florida, search out Faye and Tyler and get them. But something told me that wasn't going to be as simple as it sounded.

21. MAJOR JAMES REYNOLDS

If it had been my choice, if I were running things, Division Five wouldn't be filled up with the ones we picked up looting or causing trouble. In fact, they'd not make it into our sanctuary settlement at all.

Because most of COM Camp had moved down to the settlement before the shit hit the fan, we were able to avoid any power losses. We are the only pocket of civilization that is close to the way things were before the world shut down. At least, the only one that I know about.

The reason for placing all the troublemakers in Division Five was to keep them out of Divisions One through Four. That was the suggestion of General Allen. In a way, he had a point. If they were all kept together, as long as they had what the other divisions had, they'd stay away. Not the case—trouble was brewing constantly.

For the most part they did stay away, unless they got ill or hurt in one of the many brawls. The problem was, most of those in Division Five wouldn't work to keep things going, so those who did work would argue and fight.

My biggest concern was when, on one visit, I was asked several times if it was true that we'd found the woman. Right or wrong thing to do, I lied. Everyone knew a woman had survived; that fact ran rampant all across the settlement. It was supposed to have been kept under wraps, but all it would have taken was one person from Division Five to have been at the clinic when Faye arrived.

Leo, as he called himself, was the leader over there. It wasn't really his name; he'd stated that was his star sign, and he was putting the past, along with his name, behind him.

He was adamant that I wasn't being honest, and eventually he became abrasive and confrontational. He locked eyes with me in some sort of attempt to see if I was telling the truth. I tried to maintain eye contact, which was difficult considering I wasn't being honest. I kept telling myself that Faye depended on me. What Leo or the others would do if they knew for sure about Faye, I didn't know, and I didn't want to take a chance.

Because he was so convinced that we'd found her, I decided, just as a precaution, to check clinic records to see if anyone from Division Five was there when she arrived.

Unfortunately, someone was.

22. FAYE

It was nearly a week since I'd seen Dodge, Bud and the boys. I expected them any day, but a part of me knew Dodge's injuries were too severe for even him to bounce back in a day or two.

James had told me that using the route that had been mapped out for them, taking into account some stops, it would take them five days to get to COM Camp.

I waited impatiently.

In the meantime, James became my balcony buddy. He never sat on my side; I never invited him over, nor did he ask. I would sit outside, and after he was done working for the day, he'd come out on his patio.

Undoubtedly, he was my stand-in for Dodge.

I actually asked him to join me for my first official meeting with Barry and Dr. Lewis. Dr. Lewis was not at all what I'd expected. After meeting everyone else and experiencing how friendly they were, I was taken aback by his arrogance. He never even told me his first name.

He wasn't young like Barry Chatham. He was middle-aged, and he seemed angry at the world. He projected a smug righteousness. I wanted to tell James to smack him.

It was the end of the world as we knew it. Yet no one seemed to have told Dr. Lewis. He still wore a tie and a neat blue button-down shirt and had his hair combed perfectly. He was the type of doctor I'd always imagined solved a lot of problems and knew he was the only one who could. More than likely he'd had a trophy wife and his kids had wanted for nothing.

If arrogance had a scent, he reeked of it.

I was glad James came with me.

Nothing was said when we arrived, not at first. A younger man took four tubes of blood from me, smiled and then thanked me.

James asked him, "What are they checking for?"

"Diseases, immune deficiency. They need DNA sampling and hormone levels."

That was the one. Hormone levels.

After the blood work, I was taken to a back meeting room with a table and chairs. James and I sat down and Barry entered shortly after.

He shook our hands and was pleasant and upbeat. "How are you feeling, Faye?"

"I'm well, thank you."

"Tyler is doing wonderfully," he said.

"He'll wake soon?" I asked.

"Very. We stopped medication this morning. See? All is bright."

Then the dark hit. Dr. Lewis walked in.

He didn't introduce himself; I learned his name only because Barry said it. He pulled out a chair, dropped his folders and said, "Let's get to this."

I looked at James.

"Why is Major Reynolds here?" Dr. Lewis asked.

"I asked him," I said.

Dr. Lewis shot a serious look at James. "I certainly hope you are not breaking the rules set forth with this woman."

"Excuse me?" I said. "Rules? What rules?"

"He knows the rules," Dr. Lewis replied.

"I don't," I said.

"Doesn't matter, because he knows them. Regardless, we need to get to this right way. Enough time has been wasted since your arrival here. Let's get something straight—I don't agree with this pampered pet rule that we have with you."

I laughed. "Pampered pet?"

"You are a subject."

"No, I'm out of here." I stood up. "James." I moved toward the door.

"Stop right there, Mrs. Wills. This is out of your control."

"Bullshit," I snapped. "I came here of my own free will."

"I beg to differ." Dr. Lewis spoke calmly. "You came here because that boy needed help. He was dying. We helped him."

"Okay, thank you. But that doesn't mean I am your subject."

"You owe us."

I laughed and turned for the door.

"Time to pay the medical bills," he said. "I'll disconnect him. I will. I don't give a damn. No sweat off my back if he lives or dies. That's not why I'm here; I'm not here to save a nineteen-year-old boy, I'm here to save humanity. So make your call. Walk out that door, he gets disconnected, you get the boot. Good luck as a woman on your own out there."

I spun around. "You arrogant piece of shit." I pointed. "You have no right to talk to me like that."

"And you have no right to deny us what we need."

I laughed. "I never denied anything. I was never asked. You came in here with your holier than thou attitude, talking to me as if ... as if I were a *lab animal*. I gave my blood. What else do you need from me?"

"Your uterus."

144

I looked at Dr. Lewis, shook my head and opened the door. "You're insane," I scoffed.

"And we're out of options," Barry said passionately. "We are out of options as the human race goes. Even if you aren't the only woman, you are one of the very few left. We are facing extinction."

I slowly turned around. "I hear you. I do."

Dr. Lewis began to speak. "So you see—"

"I don't"—I flung a hand his way—"hear you!" I turned away from him and lowered my voice. "Go on, Barry."

"It's called Project Eve," Barry said. "When we first realized that it was wiping out the female population, not only was I called in to find out why, but also to find a solution. Hence the name. For those who follow the Creationist theory, they believe Adam and Eve were the first man and woman on earth. They initially bore three sons, but it's said that in their lifetime, they had something like thirty-three. In theory, if one woman bore enough female offspring, we'd have enough male children to begin repopulation."

"What is enough females?"

"Ideally, eight."

"Eight? That's absurd. Are you asking me to bear eight children, or are you thinking in terms of just taking my uterus?"

"We want you to have them. Four will suffice," Barry said. "Two sets of twins. That's all. One set, then wait a year after birth and then another."

For some reason I looked at James. He gave no indication of what he thought.

"Barry," I said, not even acknowledging the presence of Dr. Lewis, "I lost my children. It crushed me. Crushed me beyond belief. I don't know that I even want to take the chance of having and losing another child."

"I understand. That's an option; you don't even need to raise them. Give birth to them, be a surrogate only."

I took a deep breath and sat down.

"You have an obligation to do this," Dr. Lewis interjected.

"Shut up," I barked. "I don't listen to you. Barry? Even if I agreed, there's no guarantee I'd have twins, let alone females."

"Yes, there is," he replied. "I'm a geneticist. When asked to find a solution, I went immediately to the fertility clinic where I was working on genetic engineering and sex selection. I took the embryos waiting to be surrogated. We have female embryos here. Right now. Once you are primed, we implant about six. Hopefully two will take hold. If they all take hold, we will abort several for your safety and that of the children."

It was a heavy request, and one that truly went beyond what I personally wanted. I understood what they were asking. If I failed to give birth to a girl, if I truly was the last woman on earth, then was I truly failing mankind?

Was it indeed my responsibility? A part of me believed it wasn't—then there was a part of me that felt it was.

I told them with all good intentions that I needed to think about it. Honestly think it over. It was not a decision I would make lightly or impulsively.

Barry agreed to give me all the time I needed. Dr. Lewis not so much, stating, "She is playing us until the boy is healed."

When he put up a fuss about wanting an answer, James simply said, "If we hadn't found her, you'd still be waiting on an answer. So, with all due respect—stand down, Doctor."

Dr. Lewis didn't like that much, but I did.

Barry gave me the time to think it over, and I agreed to their physical examinations to determine if I could indeed be a surrogate.

I left that meeting room with a lot on my mind. Project Eve was a big responsibility. More than physically, I worried that emotionally I just didn't have it in me to handle it.

23. DODGE

"Happy Labor Day," Bud said as I walked out to the RV.

I chuckled. "What?"

"First Monday in September. Let's pause in appreciation of all your hard work."

"Thanks." I smiled, then cocked an eyebrow at him. He seemed to be dragging. "You look tired, Bud. You feeling all right?'

"Oh, I'm fine. First good night's sleep I had all week. Didn't have to get up and have inane conversations with you about carburetors, and I wasn't chasing you either."

Had Bud been the only one telling me about my odd behavior, I would have thought he was joking. But George had informed me I'd had some "spaced-out" episodes. It made sense. There were pockets of time when I'd blacked out and I didn't remember what had happened.

My head injury was worse than we'd thought. It bothered me that I was blacking out, that I was speaking gibberish, having dream-like moments that brought up high school memories.

I couldn't control my head, nor could I control my arm, which hurt far more than it should have. The air cast wasn't cutting it. My arm ached, and it was a pain worse than the headaches. Bud had suggested that maybe we needed something more stable. If we passed a clinic or hospital, we would stop and get what we needed to make a cast.

I took one hell of a beating, and I knew it. It took me nearly a week to get back to semi-normal. Bud said no way we were leaving until I made it an entire night without getting up and reliving the past.

When I woke up on Labor Day, he simply said it was time to go.

Before leaving he showed me the map the soldiers had marked. Because of the quarantine holes in the road, we had a zigzag route. We'd drive five or six hours and stop for the night. It would take five to six days to get to the Panhandle.

The boys were getting restless and bored with the KOA campsite. Darie was becoming increasingly sad. The child who barely seemed fazed by anything grew silent, and he started carrying Faye's shirt around. He insisted on being the one to hold the items Faye had left behind, constantly stating he missed her and Tyler, and he wouldn't let go of that shirt. I realized why when I tried to take it from him as we were getting ready to leave.

"Get in the RV," I said to the boys. "Darie, give me that shirt. Faye is gonna want that."

"Give it back." He handed it over.

I took it, catching a whiff of it. It made me pause.

It smelled like Faye. I brought it to my nose and took in her scent. Of course, Bud busted me doing so and asked what was wrong with me.

Nervously, I replied, "It smells like Faye."

Bud laughed, a "tee-hee" sound.

"What was that for?" I asked.

"You're funny. Kind of like a puppy dog."

"I just miss her. I miss Tyler. But I'm used to missing him, with him being off at school and all."

"Gut telling you he's fine?" Bud asked.

"Yeah, it is."

"Mine too. And we'll get to them. But then what? Have you thought beyond that? We need a long-term plan."

"Head west, I suppose. I don't know."

"Stick with the original plan. Find a good settling spot?"

"Yeah. I'm not worried about finding other survivors. I think that will come eventually as the world heals. Right now, I say we stay put and be a family, or try."

"Start all over and try to move on from the pain," Bud said.

"Yes, exactly."

"With Faye?"

I lowered my head.

"It's okay, you know. To want to move on with her. Start anew. You guys will make a heck of a family. You already do."

"You don't think her being down there will change things, do you?"

"Nah, Faye needs ya. You and her and them boys, that's what she needs. I've known Faye a lot of years. She's done a lot of healing. You did that, Dodge. The boys and you. You and her … Well, that's a given."

"I don't want to be 'the given,' Bud. I want to be 'the one.'"

"Well, isn't that just the mushiest thing I heard in years? But nice, that was nice." He grabbed the RV door and opened it. "For what it's worth, I don't think that should be a worry." He got inside.

The kids were loaded in, and I stood there. He was right. Faye and I had a connection. All I wanted was for us to be safe and away from everything.

We moved out. Our first stop wasn't far off. Even stopping for a night, that was one night closer to finding Faye and my son.

I was happy with that.

24. MAJOR JAMES REYNOLDS

The day had been pretty productive, especially being called to Division Two to meet the general, who "on the record" was none too pleased with my remark to Dr. Lewis. Off the record, he laughed. And he asked, of course, if I was breaking the rules.

I was. Not all, but some.

The rules were pretty much laid out. We were not to get personal with Faye. No soldier was to speak on a personal level to her, do anything outside the boundaries of our job. And we were not to sleep with her or make an attempt to be intimate in any way.

The rules were set forth to keep an emotional distance from her. She was one of—optimistically—a handful of surviving women. She could possibly be the only woman COM Camp would find.

But I'd broken the "personal" rules; she knew a lot about me, and I about her. Our porch talks were just that. I didn't tell the general I was breaking any of the rules, mainly because I didn't want him to switch my detail. I liked hanging out with Faye. She was a good reminder of life.

The way she moved her hands when she spoke reminded me of my wife. Her laughter brought back memories of my childhood friends. The way she drank made me think of my mother.

She was every woman I ever knew, and I valued that.

Division One was busy all day, ending up at Division Five to make four arrests after a fight broke out at their distribution center.

Rules in each section were simple. Contribute. Nothing was hard labor, but if you didn't contribute in some way, you weren't rationed your share. It was the only way to keep things running.

People didn't get that. Again, they seemed more concerned with finding the woman. That gnawed at me.

I stopped by our Post Exchange on the way home, picked up a bottle and then swung over to the mess hall. I knew I'd missed chow, but Red was working and he gave me a ton of leftovers.

After a shower, I reheated the food, grabbed my bottle and headed to the patio door.

That was when I heard it.

A child's voice, outside. I paused, wondering what a child was doing out so late. Then, as I slid open the door, I heard another voice, this one a man's.

"Hey, Faye, I'm running late, so I won't be able to swing home first. I'll still be able to grab Mark from practice though. Maybe I'll be brave and let him drive home. Love you."

Beep.

"Next message."

"Mom! Hey! Dad let me drive. I did real good. I hit the curb a couple times, but that's okay, it was my first time. So cool. Why aren't you answering? Are you sleeping? You're the best. I love you. Bye."

Beep.

My heart sank. I was so envious at that moment that I decided to retreat back into my apartment. I began to close the door.

"Wait," she called out. "Don't go. Come out."

"I didn't want to invade your privacy."

"That's your balcony."

"Are you sure?"

"Positive."

I took a step outside and paused. "Did you eat?"

"Not yet."

"I have plenty from the mess hall. Are you hungry?"

"That sounds nice. Are you sure you want to share your food?"

I just smiled, set down what I was carrying and went back inside to get her a plate.

She accepted it and said, "Smells wonderful. Is this rule breaking?"

"Probably." I sat down.

"I can't believe they set forth rules about me. How many have you broken?"

"All but one."

Faye laughed.

"Please don't let me interrupt you." I pointed to the phone.

"Are you not wanting to talk?"

"I love talking with you. I just thought ..."

"No, it's fine. I was able to charge my phones."

"Phones—as in, plural?"

"Yeah, my phone, my husband's, my son Mark's. I thought for sure after being off for so long, they wouldn't work. But lucky me. What a gift." She said it with such awe.

"It is a gift. How did you still have your phone? I thought you told me the other night you were out with friends when you went into the coma."

"I was. But that was also the time of my life when I didn't care. And this phone"—she held it up—"was put away, because I had so many pictures and videos. I was so afraid of breaking it or losing it, I didn't use it. I got one of those pay-as-you-go jobs."

"That was very smart. I am very envious. I wish I had my phone—I wish I had my wife's phone. My daughter's phone ... Well, maybe not, she was fourteen."

Faye's face crinkled. "I would be afraid to see what was on there." She paused to eat some food, and complimented it.

"They do well for us soldiers, as far as cooking."

"I'd say. Do you have pictures? Anything?"

I shook my head. "When I went down with the flu, I don't know what happened to my stuff."

"Did you go back home at all? I mean, I'm sure you had things there."

"Can I be honest?"

Faye nodded. "Please."

"I ... I've been afraid. I've been afraid to deal with that pain again."

"I understand that. Where are you from?"

"Surprisingly, about forty miles from here. Great place we got on foreclosure. Private, secluded. Beautiful."

"And you haven't gone back?"

I shook my head. "Pitiful, huh?"

"No, not at all. But you should. I'll go with you if you'd like."

"I would like that. Especially since you and I have such similar tragedies."

"Misery loves company."

With a tight smile, I shook my head again. "You're not miserable, Faye."

"No, I guess you can say I'm healing. And this helps. So you need to go get your personal items. Honestly, James, it will not hurt. It will make you smile."

I watched as she glanced down at her phone. Cautiously, I asked, "May I see your family?"

"Oh … James, yes. Please." She lifted her phone. "This is my daughter."

I leaned over the railing awkwardly, trying to glance at the small screen. "Screw it." Grabbing my food and drink, I stepped over the railing and joined Faye on her side.

"Whoa. You crossed the rail."

"I did." I sat on the chair next to her.

"Wait. Is that a rule that you broke?"

"It is." I inched closer. "But right now, I don't care."

There was something about the look she gave me. Our eyes made contact in that dim light, and she gave me the most peaceful smile. I felt it. I spent that evening looking at every single picture, listening to every story and watching every video.

Rule breaking or not, I enjoyed it.

23. FAYE

It was September eighth, Tyler had finally come out of the medically induced coma, and the next day was feeling much better. I was waiting to have an in-depth conversation with him, because I really needed to speak to him.

I had a lot on my mind, and Tyler was not only a friend, but was fast becoming a son to me. I could imagine having the conversation with my own son, Mark. He was smart and intelligent, like Tyler. He would be grown up about what I needed to discuss. I also needed to know what Dodge would think, and Tyler was my best source.

I needed to discuss my meeting with Dr. Lewis and Barry. What they had asked, not the way it had been presented, played heavily on my mind.

Tyler, of course, was a breath of fresh air. He looked so much better, and he had his color back. He was sitting up in bed, eating what looked like broth.

He smiled brightly when he saw me. "Faye, you're back."

"I am." I kissed him on the cheek, leaving my lips there an extra moment. "How are you feeling?"

"A little sore. You didn't stay long last night after I woke up."

"You needed rest."

"Faye, where am I? There are lights. There's power."

"A hospital in COM Camp, in the Panhandle community."

"I don't remember how I got here, just waking up once when they told me they were gonna operate. Before that, those guys ... They didn't hurt you, did they?"

"Nope. Your dad came."

"Where is he?"

"He's not here. He took a heck of a beating, Ty. He's up north, but hopefully will be here any day. The Army showed up looking for me right after the attack. They saved you." I pulled up a chair and sat down.

"Is my dad alright, though?"

"The medic that took care of him believes he'll be fine. We almost lost you, and that was my concern."

Tyler grabbed my hand. "Faye, you shouldn't have come here. They were searching for you. You don't know what they want."

"Actually, I do know. I need to speak to you."

"What's going on?"

"They told me what they needed. There's something called Project Eve—"

Tyler cut me off. "They want you to have babies."

My mouth tightly closed, I nodded.

"Who will be the father?"

"They already have fertilized female embryos they want to implant."

"Wow." He sat back, sinking into his pillow. "They want you to start repopulating. Breed girls so they can reproduce. That's a heck of a lot of responsibility."

"I know."

"Did they say what they were gonna do with these girl babies after they were born?"

"They want me to be a mother. But ..." I paused. "I didn't go beyond that. I think it's more of a jump-start plan."

"What did you tell them?"

"That I would think about it. Tyler, what do you think your father would say?"

"Faye, it doesn't matter. I know you and my dad have this weird post-apocalypse bond thing, but this isn't about him. It's you having the babies. What do you want to do? What are your thoughts?"

"I don't know, Tyler. I don't. Don't you think it's my obligation to do this?"

"No. No, I do not. Obligation to do what?" There was an edge to his voice. "Deliver mankind from extinction? Be the new Eve? Every species will eventually face its extinction; if it's man's turn, then there's nothing, not even carrying embryos, we can do. If man is meant to live on, then nature will find a way. Not some lab, and not by some woman made to feel guilty."

My first reaction and thought was *Wow*. This bright young man was speaking so passionately.

He'd brought up a very valid point. One I would carry with me as I made my decision.

26. DODGE

We stopped that first night at a KOA campsite Bud suggested outside of Charleston, West Virginia. We made really good time there. We saw no one on the roads at all.

But I knew the good timing thing would go to hell, because road blocks meant we had to veer off the main highway. Those pesky government-made holes made it impossible to travel. So a one-hour highway ride fast turned into a two-hour trip.

Darie didn't handle the winding roads and bumps all that well. I determined he wasn't the healthiest kid. He wasn't sickly as such, but he got sick very easily. I figured he'd never fully recovered from his bout with the virus.

Motion sickness kicked in about the same time I started hearing the clunking sound coming from the front end of the RV. I wasn't a doctor or a teacher, but I sure as heck was a good mechanic, and I knew right away it had to be the bushings or sway bar. I may not have packed the best first aid kit, but I had packed my tools. I needed a place to jack it up, take a look and do what I could to get us back on the road.

We were about ten minutes outside of a little town called Wayne. If there was one thing I learned passing through the small towns of West Virginia, it was that there may not always be a restaurant, but there almost always was an auto repair place.

My plan was to power up the shop with the generator and lift the RV. Hopefully they'd have a lift big enough, or I'd be lifting it manually with several jacks.

Wayne, West Virginia, was a hilly community with scattered frame houses, railroad tracks and a strip mall that looked like it had been abandoned long before the virus. It was a one-stoplight town with a "Population 1410" sign on the road as you drove in.

What I first believed to be a school bus graveyard ended up being a stroke of luck. It was a service shop for buses. It wasn't state of the art, but I didn't need state of the art. Fortunately, just before "town" there was a Value Auto Parts store.

It wasn't far from there to the rest of town. The courthouse peeked out at the top of the hill, just before the business district. I parked the RV outside the bus garage and decided to walk with Bud and the kids to find a good place to hunker down. I didn't know how long it would take, but being that it was already afternoon, chances were Wayne, WV, was our pit stop for the night.

We unloaded some of our things from the RV. I didn't want them staying in the shop, as it was too dirty and Darie was already susceptible to seemingly everything. The courthouse was probably the best option.

"Do we really need to fix it?" Bud asked.

"Yeah, we do. If we don't, the back roads will do us in. We're not taking the straight shot—we're going north and west and east."

"Can you fix it?"

"Can you find a KOA campsite?"

Bud laughed. He said he wanted to explore a little with the boys, and I told him to stay close. He agreed.

I headed back to the shop. I'd noticed something strange about Wayne—there were no bodies. No people lying on the streets. No cars just abandoned. In fact, the school buses were the only vehicles we'd seen.

Not a police car, aid setup or warning flyer; there was nothing that indicated the town had been hit by a virus. Nothing except the fact that there were no people.

The hydraulic lift was out and I had to go about raising the RV the old-fashioned way. Knowing all school buses came with a jack, I hit them up.

I had just raised the RV enough to crawl under when I heard an odd clomping sound. The noise was coming steadily, repeatedly, and it took a second to register—it was a trotting horse.

I stepped out of the garage and spotted Bud and the boys walking out onto the street. They must have heard it as well.

I saw it in the distance—a horse-drawn buggy. At first I wondered if we'd wandered into Amish land, especially when I saw the man riding it. He had a long beard and he wore all black. Only when he pulled closer did I notice that his clothes were some sort of robe and a hat with what looked like a veil. Closer still, I realized he also wore a cross.

He was younger, maybe thirty, and he drew the horse to a stop.

"Afternoon. We saw you arriving."

Bud and the boys had made their way over. "We?" Bud asked.

"Yes, sir." He nodded. "We have a lookout that sees for miles." He stepped down from the buggy. "I am Deacon Jeremiah." He extended his hand to me.

"My name is Dodge Cash." I indicated. "This is Bud, George, and the little one is Darie."

"Pleasure." He bowed his head slightly. "Are you in distress? The vehicle is not working?"

"It's having issues," I said. "But nothing I can't fix."

"That is good. We don't see many travelers. Most of those we do see are not traveling in recreational vehicles, nor"—he looked at Darie

166

and George—"have small children. And we wouldn't approach them; they travel the main roads."

"How many are you?" Bud asked. "You keep saying 'we.'"

"Many. Hundreds. We have not counted."

It nearly took my breath away. "Hundreds?" I sputtered.

"Yes. When news of the virus heightened, we started receiving a pilgrimage of people. We welcomed them."

"You received a pilgrimage?" I asked.

"Yes. We have a monastery ten miles into the mountains. Holy Cross Monastery. We are self-reliant in every way, and people came. We opened our gates, and we were spared, I believe, because we are remote. It never touched us."

"That's amazing," I said. "It's a pretty barren world out here."

"May I ask where you are going?"

I answered. "South. Florida."

"To the government community?" he asked.

"Not intentionally. My son was injured, and ended up there with a friend."

Darie, in his youthful naivety, blurted out, "Faye. We need to find Faye. They took her, too."

Jeremiah walked to Darie and crouched down. "That is wonderful. But God has told me something. Women like Faye are to be kept a secret." He held his finger to his mouth. "Special and protected. Do you know what that means?"

Darie nodded.

Jeremiah rubbed his head, then stood and looked at me. "If indeed this is true, then the woman, Faye, is in the hands of the government. Do you trust this?"

I shook my head. "I don't know. I honestly don't. I have to get them."

"I see. Well, while you make repairs, I offer you assistance in any way I can. The invitation is open for you to rest, have a warm bed and a meal. Also, the little one does not look well. We have a physician. I would gladly escort you there."

"Thank you, but I think—"

"Dodge," Bud interrupted. "I think we should go."

I blinked several times and held my hand up to Jeremiah. "Can you excuse us?" I took hold of Bud's arm and led him a few feet away. "We don't know them. This could be a trap."

"Well, I know of this monastery. We're in the area, and honestly, listen to the way he talks, the way he's dressed. Don't think marauders are gonna don that attire just to hijack us, do you?"

"Is it your years of gut instinct?"

"Yeah." Bud winked. "Besides, Darie ain't well. I want him to see a doctor. We don't know when we'll see another medical professional."

If Bud was thinking all was gonna be all right with this man, then I'd go with what Bud said. He did have a good gut instinct. And he was right—Darie needed to be seen by a doctor. I needed to know the boy was okay.

I asked Jeremiah if there was room for me to work on the RV at the monastery, and when he said there was, I asked if he'd wait while I did a quick assessment and gathered what I needed to fix it.

He did, and after raiding the auto parts store, I lowered the RV and followed him. We drove slowly, which worked well for the RV. It didn't clunk as badly when moving at a turtle's pace.

I knew the second we arrived at the property that we had stumbled upon something we hadn't expected.

A pickup truck was parked outside a huge gate that had to be twenty feet high. There was a wall, but I suspected it didn't go around the entire circumference of the monastery, that it was just a guarded entrance.

It took two people to open that gate for us. One of them wore a leather jacket and a baseball cap, and held a rifle; he looked like he could have been a good old boy from Wayne.

We drove through, then watched the gates close behind us.

The road was narrow, but it opened up after a mile. While we had not yet arrived at the main area of the monastery, we did see something else.

Trailers, RVs, tents, all set up—and more than those, we saw people.

A lot of people. They didn't look like refugees. They appeared to be moving about as a community. Some were doing laundry, some were cooking. I saw men working on a construction project.

Our pace slowed down even more when a child darted across the road; he was followed by two pigs.

Chickens and other livestock moved about freely, as if they were just as much a part of the community as everyone else.

"Good God," Bud gasped. "This is a sanctuary."

"Look, Darie," George said, excited. "Kids—we can play. Can we play with them, Dodge? Can we?"

"Yeah," I murmured. "Sure." I barely blinked as I drove, taking it all in. Jeremiah hadn't been exaggerating when he said hundreds had flocked there in pilgrimage.

"Dodge, this is the place," Bud said. He sounded slightly shocked. "You have to get Faye—this is where you settle. There is life here. It's safe here."

While I wasn't certain it was where I wanted to settle, Bud was correct in stating there was indeed life, and that it was safe. The monks and those who had traveled there had made it safe. They had to.

I was rendered speechless, but grateful, because speckled throughout the masses of survivors were women of all ages.

Faye was not the last one.

27. FAYE

Several things transpired that afternoon when Tyler took his first steps post-surgery. We ran into Barry, who asked if I could take some tests. Since Tyler was worn down from his brief but productive walk, I agreed.

Barry didn't ask me if I had decided, but it had been a couple days and I know he wanted to.

I hadn't made up my mind, but the subject was heavy on my thoughts.

Should I? Shouldn't I?

My blood work had come back perfect, and I agreed to an ultrasound. That was immediate, and the results stated I was fit for pregnancy.

Those tests were nothing compared to Barry asking if they could start the in vitro, frozen embryo transfer injection process.

I was clueless as to what that meant, and Barry explained that when dealing with cryogenically frozen embryos, the uterus needs to be prepared for implantation. There was only a fifty percent chance that it would work, hence why he wanted to implant six embryos.

"Why do you want to give me injections if I haven't made up my mind?" I asked.

"Because that way, if you decide to do so, your body is ready. Right now it's perfect timing because you just finished your cycle."

"What happens if I decide against it?"

"Nothing, you'll continue on. You may miss a period, but nothing drastic."

The tests took most of the afternoon, and fortunately I did not run into Dr. Lewis.

I had so many questions about COM Camp since it had dawned on me that I knew of only our division and the bad one, and nothing about the others. It was something that I had never asked James about in all our conversations. It came up now because Barry stated that should I conceive, I would have to be monitored constantly. Not hooked up to anything, but staying within the division.

Did I want that? The idea of permanent residency at COM Camp was now a factor in my decision.

Was it indeed a place where I wanted to raise children, if I actually kept them?

I couldn't see Dodge or even Bud wanting to stay there. Tyler hadn't seen enough to formulate an opinion.

I did finally find someone else that would speak to me about COM Camp—the male nurse who was taking care of Tyler.

He said it was against the rules, but offered some information. Primarily children were kept with caretakers in Division Two. Division Three was farming, and Division Four was mainly housing for those who worked in other divisions.

I asked him if he liked it.

He hesitated, then said, "It's better than surviving out there."

I didn't get that. I was fine with surviving out there. Dodge had it down. We just needed a new place to start. Then again, perhaps things were different for those traveling the roads. Look at what happened to us when we ventured from my house.

My day was pretty bland—about the most exciting thing was getting that cold gel squirted on my stomach for the test. I couldn't walk around, I couldn't see the division. There was a rumor that the president wanted to meet me, but that had yet to happen.

Either I prepared my meals or they were brought to me. I went where they said I could go and stayed where they told me to stay.

I was just as much a secret in Division One as I was out in the world, the only difference that outside, the world was better. In a sense, I was free out there.

Air-conditioning, clean surroundings, protection, food and hot water. Most of those things I would eventually have again with work.

They weren't motivation enough to make me want to stay in COM Camp. Because unfortunately, more than I realized or James believed, I was nothing more than a well-kept prisoner.

28. DODGE

Life seemed simple, if only for that day. There was something about being on the monastery grounds that brought out the best in everyone. Everyone but me, of course.

But I didn't really care much. My focus was on three things. Make sure Darie was well, fix the RV and go get Faye and Tyler.

Firsts things first. Jeremiah took us to the doc, as he was called—the doctor who had lived in Wayne before all hell broke loose. He took a look at my air cast and said that it wasn't going to do, and he wanted to set it properly. I knew a cast would take hours to dry, so I opted to work on the RV first. As he examined Darie, he told of how there had been only three instances of the sickness on the monastery grounds. But the way they handled it was sniffles and cold, flu or not, they were isolated. Jeremiah said they had been spared; the doc clarified that, telling us not a single monk had been ill.

Of the fourteen hundred in Wayne, two hundred had retreated immediately to the holy grounds. Another third left, and then many more just trickled in. Half the people of Wayne they couldn't account for; the doc believed they had died.

He gave Darie a good exam, asking him a million questions, then asking me the same. He didn't have the resources to do blood work, so he had to rely on knowledge, old-fashioned wives' tale signs, deduction and reasoning.

Darie was not dying, as Bud had put into my head. He wasn't well, the doc said. Not only was he undernourished, he was pining for Faye. He missed her terribly, telling the doc that she was helping to be a mom because his mom had died.

Admittedly, I was a little jealous. I took care of those boys, or at least all the dirty work, and Faye got all the glory and love.

Yeah, I suppose they loved me, or liked me a lot. But I highly doubted either of those boys would get sick from not being around me.

Despite the fact that we had food, Darie hadn't eaten much. I knew that. I'd tried. But it wasn't like we could claim defeat, pull into McDonald's and get the child an order of nuggets that we knew he'd devour.

The old adage—if they're hungry, they'll eat—didn't hold true in this instance.

The doc told us we had to try anything and everything to get some nourishment in him. I decided then that I didn't give a shit if it was candy—that child was getting calories. When we resumed our journey there would be plenty of stores to raid.

Following the exam, the boys said they wanted to play with the other kids, and I took advantage of that time to jack up the RV and get to work on it.

One would have thought I was some sort of engineering guru, the way people came over to talk to me while I worked. Asking if I knew how to fix this or that, and telling me how they were glad they had someone with "fix it" knowledge. Some even said I had to be a master, doing it all with a bum arm.

It was hard to tell them I wasn't staying, but for some reason, they were all like, "You'll be back."

Even with the distractions, not to mention the pain in my arm, I finished the RV in a couple hours and set her to the ground. That was going to be our home for the night.

Admitting defeat, I sought the doc. I popped a pain pill and he set my arm. I don't know if it was the plaster cast and my arm being set right or the pill, but for the first time since I was beaten up, my arm didn't hurt so badly.

After the cast had had time to dry, I went back outside. Darie and George were still darting about. I could tell Darie didn't feel a hundred percent, but he wasn't missing the chance to play with new kids or to tail his brother around.

Bud had built us a small fire and sat facing the boys, watching them play like a proud grandfather.

"Is that coffee?" I asked, making myself comfortable in the folding chair next to him.

"Yeah, pretty good too. How's my Fastball?"

"Good, I think. I'll know once we get her on the road."

"That's reassuring."

"Trust me." I winked. "I know what I'm doing."

Darie squealed loudly and I looked up. I didn't know if it was a happy or scared noise, but when I saw the smile, I knew he was fine.

"Probably feeling that energy," Bud said. "Or gas. One of the two is making him laugh."

"What are you talking about?"

"While you were fixing Fastball, that boy ate."

"He ate? What did he eat?"

"One of them monks cooked up some kettle beans. Big old kettle over a fire. Molasses, I think was in them, not sure. So thick you didn't even know they were beans. Darie ate two large bowls."

"Darie ate beans? I tried to feed him beans."

"That's because you opened a can. You didn't roast them over a fire."

"Actually, I would have loved to try them."

"They brought you a helping."

"They did?"

"Yeah, but Darie ate them. Ate mine too. Figured if he was eating, he could have them. We have food, so no worries."

"I'm not." I rubbed my hands together, reaching out toward the fire. It was getting cooler.

"This is nice here, Dodge. Really nice."

"I don't know."

"You don't know?" Bud asked. "Look around."

"Do you trust it?"

Bud laughed. "Monks are running this place. And I wouldn't exactly say they were running it, just providing. People here are good. One man was telling me they have little tunnels under the cabins. They have drills to move the women there in case anything happens."

I shook my head. "Just not what I want."

"Well, what the hell then, Dodge? You want a place to settle. You thought about joining the Kentucky people. You yourself said you want the boys to have people around them. Well, here it is."

"Things change, Bud."

"Like what?"

"Like Faye ... and women in general. Hiding in a catacomb at the first sign of trouble. I think she stands a better chance being off somewhere secluded."

"What about them boys? What kind of life are they going to have? Or Tyler. They need people around them. You may not, but they do."

"What about you?"

Bud exhaled loudly. "You know, when all this happened, and my wife died, my kid died, I wandered like Faye. Not wanting to live. I figured, heck, how much time do I actually have? Not giving out my age, and not that you'd know it 'cause I'm a handsome fella, but I'm over eighty."

That surprised me. I hadn't known. Faye believed he was in his seventies, maybe. Bud looked good. "You still have some years, Bud."

"Yeah, I do. So it doesn't matter where I wind them down. Here, there, back home. Rolling down the broken road in Fastball. Doesn't matter. But I'll be honest with you; I also wouldn't mind pulling back Fastball some. Parking right over there by the edge of the trees." He pointed. "And hanging here, watching them boys. This is God's green earth as best as you can define it. It would be good staying here until it's my time. But I go where you go."

"Thank you."

"You *are* using my RV."

That made me laugh. "I think I just have a problem with joining an already established community. Sort of like I'd be just a sheep here."

"That's the control freak in you talking. But I see your point. I do think before you make any decision to go off with the kids, start your own Monk City, you should talk to Faye. We're all like a family, and this should be a family decision. Not a Dodge choice."

"You're right," I said. "Man. How did you get so wise, Bud?"

"I'm old. You know that. Wait. You may not. My good looks hide my age."

I chuckled and stood, in the mood for a cup of coffee myself. I headed toward the RV to make a cup and some food. Probably wouldn't be anywhere as good as the coffee Bud had or the beans that Darie had eaten, but I'd make do.

I glanced over my shoulder to Bud, who had resumed watching the boys. Then I looked at the boys; they were playing some sort of catch and release game, and their laughter filled the air.

Tyler popped into my mind, and my heart skipped a beat as I hoped and prayed that my son was fine. I wondered what Faye was doing and if she would really enjoy the monastery sanctuary as much as Bud, or if she would be like me and just want to be on our own.

Soon enough I'd find out. In the morning we'd leave. I'd let them know that we'd be back, even if it was just for a brief visit.

Besides, I actually wanted to know about the camp down in Florida. Maybe they offered even more. I watched the boys for another minute and slipped into the RV.

Maybe the whole reason nothing felt right was that Faye wasn't there. She was a new addition to my life that had appeared when everything went bad. Every decision made was together, every meal, every evening conversation. In the four months since we'd met, we'd barely been apart for more than a couple hours. Now, it had been a week, and it was driving me nuts.

No decision could be made or even contemplated until we were all together as a unit. Hopefully the unity of our group wasn't that far off.

29. FAYE

More than likely it was my paranoia or even my overactive, Hollywood-induced imagination, but I was certain that injection they gave me to prepare my uterus was some super-hormone concoction designed to make fertilization infallible. After all, this was the lab that had injected me in the name of a project called Eve.

A soup of hormones typically used in frozen embryo implantation was how Barry described it. He told me that in the pre-virus world, many women undergoing in vitro had received it. It was one of three injections needed.

I didn't buy that. There was something off about the injection; it sent my body and mind into a tailspin. I was hot, then cold. Sick to my stomach and achy, my breasts hurt then they didn't. I was angry that it was humid, then I cried when I saw a flower.

I told James I didn't like how I felt. That something was off.

He suggested that I was tired and that was magnifying everything. That made sense—everything always seemed worse when I was tired—so even though it was early evening I decided on a nap.

Jokingly, I said to James, "If you don't see me later, come check on me to make sure I didn't die."

He didn't laugh.

My nap wasn't long, but it was a hard sleep and one I wish I hadn't taken. The hormones that were intensifying my emotions seeped into my dream and it became a nightmare.

A nightmare I had lived.

My subconscious released the reasons why I didn't want to have another child, and in the dream I lived it.

I dreamt of that fateful day when I lost my family.

In the dream I watched them die. I watched our SUV get smashed by that truck, flip in the air and ricochet off four cars. I saw the impact on the passenger side clearly, killing Rich instantly and sending my daughter, Sammy, from her Youth Seat out of the vehicle and onto the street, right where they had found her.

I screamed and cried and woke up feeling that pain all over again.

It was with me always, but had dulled since the accident. Now, with that dream, it returned with a vengeance. So much so I grabbed my chest, struggling to breathe, convinced I was having a heart attack. I stood, legs wobbling, reaching out to the darkened room, and then I knew I wasn't having a heart attack; I wasn't lucky enough to die. I was alive, reliving that day all over again and feeling the heartache. An emotional pain so deep and so real, it manifested physically.

It was traumatic. I dropped to my knees and sobbed. My babies. My husband. My entire existence died that day.

What was I doing? Suddenly all the healing I had experienced over the previous seven months vanished.

I was a mere shell of existence, crumbling on the floor of the apartment.

Never again in my entire life did I want to lose someone I loved so much.

The dream, I believe, was the answer to the question I had been debating.

When Rich and the kids were taken from me, I shut down to everyone. Letting Dodge, the boys and Bud into not only my life but also my heart was opening myself up to experiencing that pain again. I had already gambled with that. Getting impregnated, having a child, would just increase the likelihood of further heartache and loss.

Crying uncontrollably, hands to my face, I realized I wasn't yet ready to take that chance. I wasn't ready emotionally to think about having a child. Not yet. Maybe in the future, maybe when I was stronger, but it was still too soon.

For now, I knew what my decision was—and I feared how Dr. Lewis would react when I told him my answer was definitely no.

30. DODGE

Darie had this keen ability to twist and turn his body in the smallest of places. We stayed in the RV, and while I debated sleeping in the driver's seat, I opted for the covered sofa, which folded out into a wider, twin-size bed. Bud insisted it was a double.

It wasn't one of those luxury, extra-long RVs, but it was a nice size. Because it was Bud's he got the rear queen bed.

George opted for the other couch without pulling it out. Surprisingly, the boys were asleep early. I took advantage of that and decided to sleep as well. After all, I wanted to get an early start. So when Darie's foot plowed into my face, I took the upside-down restless sleeper as my personal alarm clock and got up.

It was starting to get light and I illuminated my watch. Six-thirty.

I was surprised I'd slept that long. My arm felt nearly one hundred percent better, no hard morning ache shooting up my bicep. While the plaster short cast was heavier, it was actually easier for me to move, less awkward.

I sat up on the bed and Darie shifted again. I ran my hand over his head then adjusted him on the pillow and covered him. I smiled; he'd fallen asleep with Faye's shirt.

I got up and checked on George, who had barely moved since the night before. The scent of something cooking outside carried into the RV, along with the smell of coffee. I decided to go seek out a cup—maybe someone would be neighborly.

But first I wanted to get dressed. When we left the KOA campsite following my recovery, we packed everything pretty tight, putting things in the order we'd need them. Extra food and water was carried in the overhead storage.

My plan had been to take a few moments in the morning, get mentally prepared, wake the crew, get them fed, and then we'd be on our way. Maybe push for a longer traveling day. To maximize space, most of our stuff was tucked away in some nook or cupboard, but our clothes were in the back room.

I hated to disturb Bud, so I put on the small wall light in the hall outside the queen room, quietly slid open the door as little as possible and slipped in.

My duffle bag was on the floor near the foot of the bed. Matching or not, I would reach in, grab a shirt and a new pair of pants. Careful not to make a noise, I slowly unzipped the bag and reached in. I grabbed a T-shirt, felt for denim and tugged out a pair of jeans. I'd fix the items later. I just wanted to get my things and get dressed.

For the life of me, I couldn't feel socks so opted against them. As "gross" as Faye would claim that to be, she wasn't with us and I would go another day without socks.

As I stood with the slightest of grunts, I noticed a hint of light cast upon Bud as he slept in the bed. My heart skipped a beat, as it always did when I saw his eyes were open.

I laughed, shaking my head. "Damn it, Bud, I hate when you do that."

With another chuckle, I reached for the door, but paused when I didn't get a response.

Typically, when Bud was awake and quiet, he would make a sarcastic comment.

But Bud was silent.

A lump formed in my throat. The word barely squeaked out of my mouth; it was caught somewhere in my closed-up throat. "Bud?"

Silence.

I felt a twitch in my gut and my hand trembled some as I reached for the door. I opened it wider to bring more light into the room.

Bud was lying on his side, one arm tucked under his head, the other draped across and dangling down the edge of the bed. It was his typical sleeping position, and he looked peaceful. His eyes were open.

I walked to the bed.

An ache crept up my chest and seeped out as a soft moan. "Oh, Bud." I breathed out heavily, immediately taken with a sense of loss. I reached down to him. His right arm had the appearance of settled blood, and when I touched his head, his skin was cool.

Standing there, I was at a loss, and it struck me how big a hit this was going to be. The boys wouldn't comprehend it, and Faye was going to be crushed.

Truth was, so was I.

I ran my fingers gently across his face, closing his eyes, then I took a moment. A private moment to say my own goodbye to a man I had grown to know and love.

Bud was gone.

31. FAYE

I fell asleep just before dawn and slept only a couple hours. My headache was better and I wasn't crying, but I could feel the seesaw mood swings creeping up on me as I made my first cup of coffee of the morning.

I hadn't slept much the night before, and I was curious as to where James had gone. He never came out on the balcony; his lights never turned on. The last I'd seen him was when I had my late lunch and injection.

My guard said he'd had matters to attend to, and that was all I was told.

This was to be Tyler's last day in the hospital. If he was strong enough they'd let him out. I'd bought him time by not giving my answer.

I honestly, seriously, had given it deep thought. More than I'd have thought I would.

I loved my children, Mark and Sammy. Loved them more than I loved life itself. They completed me, and without them I wasn't the same. A part of me longed to have that love again. To hold a child and have my chest just fill with emotions that couldn't be brought on by anything else.

That was love. The unconditional love a mother has for her child.

With that love came the chance of heartache. Heartache that I was not alone in experiencing. Mine was just different.

Perhaps the injection had fueled some sort of unreasonable emotional response. I did take that into account.

As I sipped my coffee I was hit with an overwhelming sense of loss. I missed the boys, Dodge and Bud. I actually laughed when I looked at my choices for breakfast and one of them was Spam. I swore Dodge had wanted to lose it every time I suggested Spam. But he was patient, nodded and went with the flow.

In my heart I knew he'd healed from the attack, but with the days that had passed I started to worry. Where were they? Surely, even if— God forbid—something had happened to Dodge, Bud would have brought the boys to me. James had told me he'd made it a point to give good directions.

I worried that something was wrong, that something had happened; they should have arrived at COM Camp by now.

Just as I was about to decide on a meal, a knock came at the door. I honestly knew it could only be one person—James.

I called out for him to come in, and he entered holding a plate.

"Hey, they had pancakes at the mess hall," James said. "Thought you might want some."

The plate was covered with a cloth. I lifted it, and they looked wonderful. "Thank you."

"How are you?" he asked. "I heard the balcony doors slide, figured you were out here like you always are."

"I wasn't feeling all that great, not to mention I felt like I had the worst case of PMS ever."

"You'll have that when they give you a hormonal cocktail. Which I told you I don't trust. I don't get why they had to rush that."

"I don't either." I reached down and broke off a piece of pancake. "Was there trouble last night? You weren't around."

"Nah. Things I wanted to take care of." He shrugged. "Are you feeling better?"

"Yes. But I had a rough night. Thoughts of my kids, my husband. You know."

"I do."

I brought the pancake to my mouth, enjoying it for a moment, and then looked at James. "I'm not gonna do it."

"Excuse me?"

"I can't. I can't do it right now. I thought about it and—"

"Faye, you don't have to explain your reasons to me."

"I know," I said. "But I have them. It's not that I am ruling out a child. I'm just not ready to have one now. If I am meant to have a child, I think I'll leave that up to fate and not science."

"Whatever you want to do. Remember that."

"How do you think they'll react?"

James took a loud breath. "Honestly, I don't know."

"Are they gonna kick me out? Not that I care, but Dodge is on his way down and I don't want him to get here and I'll be gone. He'll never find me."

"That's not going to happen."

"You mean they won't make me leave."

"I don't know about that," James said. "I'm referring to Dodge. He'll find you no matter what."

"How can you be so sure?" I was feeling a little panicked. After all, it was a worry to me. I had his son; I knew and felt that Dodge was on his way. We were a partnership that I didn't want apart any longer. "We can't be sure."

"Yes, I can. I was thinking ahead. If they make you leave ..." He winked. "Trust me. I have a plan."

31. DODGE

The last thing I wanted to do was wake up the boys and tell them that Bud had passed away in his sleep. That would be a hell of a thing to wake up to.

I didn't want to leave the RV at all; it wasn't a chance I wanted to take. I hated the thought of George waking up and finding Bud.

When I heard voices outside, soft enough not to wake the boys, I quietly crept from the RV and signaled the two men to come over.

After alerting them to stay quiet, I asked if one of them could pass on to those in the monastery that I needed some help; my friend had died.

They looked as if they too had lost a friend. Their heads hung low, they conveyed their sympathies and said they'd let Deacon Jeremiah know.

I had to think about how I would tell the boys. When they stirred less than an hour later, I had their breakfast ready. Granola, some fruit snacks and juice.

"Jeremiah said he'd give us eggs today," George said. "How come we're not having eggs?"

"I didn't feel like going to the monastery to eat," I replied, sitting at the table with them. Darie didn't seem to mind. He picked at his food. Although I bet he would rather have had eggs.

"How come Bud's not up with us?" George asked.

"Is he still sleeping?" Darie said.

"He's in bed," I replied.

George laughed. "Is Bud being lazy today? He's never the late sleeper. We should get him for breakfast. Bet he'd want to go to the monastery."

"Stay here and eat," I told him.

"Why don't you want us to get Bud? You mad at him?"

I shook my head. "No, I'm not mad at Bud." I cleared my throat. "Not at all."

George gave me a sideways glance. "You sick? Hurt?"

"Me? No."

"You look it. You look pale. We should get Bud."

"Stay here."

"Darie, run and wake up Bud."

Darie stood, but I held out a hand to stop him. "Just eat, please."

"You're being rude, Dodge. You can't let Bud sleep through breakfast. That's not nice." George stood up. "I'll get him."

Before I could react, George darted toward the back of the RV. It took all of my agility to stop him.

"What is wrong with you?" George asked. "You're being weird."

I crouched down and stared at him seriously. "Please," I said softly. "Go sit down. I'll tell you."

And then I did.

Their reactions weren't what I had expected. Darie was a little scared, I think more so because Bud was still in the back room.

"Is he gonna get up like me and Faye?" Darie asked.

"No. No, he's gone."

I expected sadness from George. I suppose he was, but the very mature child showed nothing but anger. He asked if he could see Bud, and after some debate, I let him. I tried to stand in the doorway, but he asked me to leave. I don't know what happened in that back room, but when he emerged he ran right out.

Jeremiah wasn't far; in fact he was just outside the RV, as if he'd been waiting. He stood when George took off running. I went to chase him, but Jeremiah stopped me.

"Lyle's following him," he said. "The boy needs to absorb this. To him and us, everyone finished dying months ago. This is a big deal."

My hand shot to my face. I wanted to scream. I couldn't believe Bud was gone. "It's a big deal to me, too."

"I'm sorry for your loss. For all of you." Jeremiah reached out and laid a hand on my shoulder. "I had time to speak to Bud. He was a man of faith, and knowing that, I would like to handle his burial properly."

I slowly dragged my fingers across my face. "What do you mean?"

"We have a cemetery here. I'll have two men get a spot ready, and we'll have a service for him this afternoon."

I guess, in my shock, I didn't handle that well. It didn't make sense, and I was confused. "Why?"

"Why?" Jeremiah gave an emotional chuckle. "My friend, part of what makes us civilized is how we deal with our dead. This world was besieged with sickness so fast that we as a civilization put asunder all that we knew and did. The goodbye, the ceremony of burial, were forgotten. There were too many, too fast, and we tossed them like garbage into mass graves. Human beings deserve more respect than to be discarded. Those were people that were loved. But the problem was, those who loved them died along with them. Not now. Mr. Doyle has you and the boys. If we intend to be civilized and human again, we must return to all practices, and that includes burying our dead with dignity."

He was right. Though what to do with Bud's remains wasn't really a thought for me at that moment. I was too busy worrying about the boys and how Faye and Tyler were going to react.

I agreed and thanked Jeremiah. He informed me that he would handle the arrangements and I was to take care of the boys.

That was a lot.

Darie was sitting on Bud's folding chair, and George returned a short time later, kicking his feet as he walked.

"You all right?" I asked.

"No. No. It's not fair."

"I know."

He put his hands in his pockets and looked up at me. "Where is he? He still inside?"

I shook my head. "No, Jeremiah and a couple of the brothers took him. He'll be buried here in the cemetery."

"What!" George cried. "You let them take him?"

"Yes, George. We're going to have a funeral."

"And leave him here?"

"That's what a funeral is," I said.

"I know what a funeral is, Dodge." It seemed the angrier and more emotional George grew, the more his Georgia accent came out. "But they took Bud and you wanna leave him here. You can't leave him here."

"What do you want me to do? Tie him to the top of the RV and roll to Florida like that?"

"Yes." George nodded. "'Cause it's his RV. This is his journey. We're his family. He deserves to be there when we find Faye."

"George, that's not realistic."

"Yes, it is. It's the right thing to do."

"Do you think Bud would want that?" I asked. "He wouldn't. He said to me yesterday that this was the place he wanted to live his last days. Well, he did. As sad as that makes us, as angry as it makes us, there is nothing we can do about it."

George sniffled. I heard it and saw it on his face, but he was so stubborn and thrown by Bud's passing that he wouldn't give in to the sadness or want me see it. He scowled at me. "Fine. Nothing we can do about it. But we can do something about Faye and Tyler. Go get them. I want us all back together."

"We will be. As soon as—"

George cut me off as he stormed by me to the RV. "As soon as we can. Fast too." He opened the door, then paused. He looked so sad, with a pout to his lips. When he spoke again the anger was gone. "Please," he said, his voice small. "Please, I need Faye."

He lowered his head and slipped inside the RV.

I exhaled, trying to relieve some of the heaviness I felt. It didn't work. George was a little boy carrying a man-sized heartache.

There was nothing I could do to ease the pain of Bud's death. But I would do everything I could to get George and Darie not only on the road to feeling better emotionally, but on the road to getting our family back together.

32. FAYE

Tyler looked the best I had seen him in a while. Even before the injury. His color had returned, and maybe he'd been given the nutrients he'd been missing, I didn't know. But his smile was brighter, and he was playing a video game when I walked into his room. No longer was he hooked up to machines; only the shunt remained in his arm.

It was a welcome sight, and I knew he was going to be leaving the hospital soon.

My early morning talk with James hadn't bred any answers as to what I would do if they asked us to leave, but he'd been certain all would be fine.

That changed when he received a request from the president to lead the escort team to Washington, DC. All that James could tell me was that it involved important government documents along with personal items.

The escort would be gone two nights. He was nervous, and asked me not to say anything about my decision until he returned. To me,

James was going a little overboard on what "they" might do when they found out I wouldn't be bearing a child just yet.

I gave him my word. I hated living under the false pretense that I was still making a decision, but the two days gave him time to return or for Dodge to get here.

Dodge.

The boys.

Even though I had the comforts of my old life, I wanted that simple life with Dodge, Bud and the boys.

Not surprisingly, Tyler asked about them the second I stepped into the room. "Any word at all?"

"Not yet."

He looked down at his game controller and then back at me. "You don't think my dad didn't make it, do you?"

"You mean, do I think your dad died?"

Tyler nodded.

"No," I said with the utmost certainty. "I don't feel it. I think about Dodge, and I feel he's fine. Not like I'm psychic, but we developed a bond. Something is holding them up."

"Like what?"

"Car trouble, maybe."

"Can't be car trouble," Tyler scoffed. "My dad is like the master mechanic."

"Okay, well, then something else." I pulled up a chair. "Dodge is fine. They're fine. I just … I just wished they'd get here."

"You don't wanna stay?" Tyler asked.

"As much as this is really great, having electricity, I feel like I lost my sense of freedom."

"I'm feeling better—we can go when he gets here."

"I'm looking forward to it." I grabbed his hand.

"How are you?"

"Me? I'm fine. I had a rough night. The hormone injection was like a bad night of drinking, and I know those." I faked a laugh. "But …" I exhaled. "I won't be getting another one."

"Why? Was one enough?"

"For now. However, I think I'm going to let nature take its course."

"What do you mean?"

"I just don't know that I am ready to be the new Eve."

A voice entered the room. It wasn't one that I'd have expected. It was Dr. Lewis. "Is that your final decision?"

Surprised, I turned in the chair then stood.

"I heard you speaking. Is that your decision?" he asked, his voice emotionless.

"Listen, Dr. Lewis. I know the timing of my decision with Tyler getting well and all is … It probably looks like I strung you along. But I honestly thought about it. I really did. I looked at pictures of my kids on my phone. I thought of the good memories. I gave it every thought."

"I see."

He stared at me as if waiting for me to say something else. Perhaps to sputter out my reasoning. As I prepared to do just that, I saw rushing movement in the hall and heard voices.

Dr. Lewis looked over his shoulder to the commotion, and then, as if it didn't faze him, he returned his attention to me. I expected him to tell me to get Tyler and go, to leave immediately. I was ready for that.

"May I speak to you alone?" he asked. "Please."

Please? Dr. Lewis—the arrogant, unaffected, unemotional doctor—said *please?*

I nodded, then glanced back at Tyler before following Dr. Lewis to the door.

We stopped as a soldier raced past us. "What's going on?" I asked.

"Trouble with one of our divisions." He led the way down the hall.

"Division Five?"

He stopped, looked at me and shook his head, almost in disgust. "Yes, I suppose Major Reynolds told you about them."

Immediately, I thought back to how concerned James had been about that division. Almost like a kid waiting for their parents to go out of town, it seemed Division Five had waited until James wasn't around. "He told me a little. Why are the soldiers running?"

"We're having some problems with them at our gate."

"They're really rushing."

"There are a lot out there." He turned the bend. "Nothing you should worry about. We have it under control." He stopped at a closed door. "This is my office. Come in." He opened the door. "We need to talk."

My heart beat a little faster. Walking in there was like walking into the boss' office when something was wrong. I had a bad feeling about what he was going to say, and a part of me was afraid.

Even though I didn't trust him, didn't want to go into that room with him, I owed him my time at least. I stepped inside his office and he closed the door.

33. DODGE

The monks at the Holy Cross Monastery did a nice job for Bud's final send off. Bud would have liked it. Two of the men went into Wayne and collected a coffin from the local mortuary. Coffins hadn't been used during the virus. The ceremony of a funeral added a sense of closure, and the entire community attended the service then walked to the cemetery with the coffin, which was carried in a horse-drawn buggy.

It was followed by a late lunch of bread and soup. Darie ate his food, while George picked at it. The eldest of the boys was fussy and agitated.

Though sad, Darie had taken Bud's passing gracefully. He acknowledged the loss and spoke highly of Bud, while never letting go of Faye's shirt.

Faye was going to have to launder that T-shirt when all was said and done.

It was pushing 4 p.m. by the time everything was finished. We still had a few hours of daylight left for traveling, and by my calculations still twelve hours of travel to go until we reached the government camp.

I was ready to pack up and go, but Deacon Jeremiah thought it was best we spend one more evening. His reasoning was we couldn't pull into that camp at night, and we were still two nights' rests away from getting there whether we left immediately or waited until dawn.

"Get rest, rejuvenate the spirit, leave at dawn and push extra in traveling. The little one is better now, he'll handle it."

It made sense, but George had been obstinate about leaving immediately. But because Jeremiah was the one to ask, he reluctantly agreed to stay one more night.

Jeremiah made another suggestion—leave the RV, go into town and find a smaller and easier means to travel to Florida. I was a mechanic, so I could make sure any car was roadworthy.

"Leaving Bud's RV here is not in the cards," I told him. We were sitting outside it.

"You are returning."

"Not for long."

"Even then, leaving it is a sensible decision. The RV and your belongings will be safe."

I held up my hand. "I know that. I do."

"The RV is big, it requires a lot more stops to refuel. You want to make the trip quickly—you won't do that with a thirty-two-foot recreational vehicle."

"I'll think about it."

"And I can't convince you to leave the youngest here?" Jeremiah asked. "Until you return?"

"No." I shook my head. "Faye will kill me if I show up down there without Darie."

Jeremiah nodded. "I understand that. But he's so little, and he's running and playing."

I looked up to see Darie playing with another child. "I see that. But he has to go."

"Can I ask why you are so adamant about not joining the community here?"

Before I could answer, George pulled up a chair and sat with us. He answered for me. "Because Dodge thinks this is a cult."

It wasn't the answer I would have given. Although, as brazen and blunt as he said it, there was a distorted truth in George's words.

Jeremiah quickly looked at me. "We are not a cult."

"I didn't say that," I said.

"Did too," George said. "Bud told me you called it a cult. Said you told him that all the men were gonna have to grow long beards and be monks and the women—"

"Stop. I said no such thing. Bud was lying."

George gasped. "Why would Bud lie?"

"Because Bud liked to tell tales." I then looked at Jeremiah. "I didn't say it was a cult. I did express reservations about this being a monastery."

"I see. Well, we are not a cult. Yes, this land once was a monastery, but it's God's land. These people here are a community. We don't force them to follow our beliefs. The only rules we have are to respect the land and the others. Be good to one another. We're trying to rebuild here, Dodge. A safe environment. Because it's not safe out there. Especially for women."

"Don't we know that," George said. "That's why Faye isn't here. The men wanted her because she was a woman."

"Hundreds of people here," Jeremiah said. "Some are female. The virus was not kind to women. We need to protect them and keep them safe. Here they are. Out there, it's hiding and running. It will only get worse."

I heard his words and agreed. "Jeremiah, it's not that I don't want Faye safe. I just wanted us to go somewhere new and start again."

"And then what?" Jeremiah asked. "What about the boys? How will that aid them growing up, not being around anyone else? We remain—it is up to us to rebuild. All the means are here. God—"

Sometimes George was too mature for his own good. He didn't even let Jeremiah finish before he spouted out, "There is no God."

I cringed a little. But Jeremiah wasn't thrown. Calmly, he asked George, "You don't believe in God?"

"Nope."

"Did you ever?"

George nodded. "Yep. I did. I believed when I was praying really hard. Praying for God to save my mom and dad. But He didn't. I'm sure everyone was praying. But God didn't answer anyone's prayers. Know why? Because there isn't a God. I figure, if there was one, He'd answer prayers."

"God can't answer everyone's prayers. And sometimes prayers are answered differently."

"It's a dead world," George said.

"I beg to differ," Jeremiah said. "Look around. All around is life. I am sorry that God didn't answer your prayer, but He did answer prayers."

"How can you say that?"

"Because I can bet my life your mother and your father were praying that you and Darie would live. While she was ill, she wasn't praying for herself, she was praying for you. I believe God answered that prayer. Dodge prayed for his children. His son lives. I am sure Bud's children prayed for him. He lived."

"What about Faye?" George asked. "Who prayed for her? No one. Her kids died long before the sickness, her husband too. She don't have a mom or dad. Or family. She was out cold, laying in a mound of bodies. Who prayed for her?"

"Just because Faye lived, doesn't mean someone wasn't praying for her. Maybe she was chosen. Maybe, because the doctors of the world knew this virus was wiping out the female population, maybe there was one doctor out there praying that one woman lived. Maybe Faye was that one woman answered in his prayers." Jeremiah reached out and grabbed George's hand. "We don't know. I can't convince you there is a God. I can convince you without a doubt there is life. This isn't a dead world. Not yet." He stood slowly, running his hand over George's head, and then glanced outward. "I think I'll go play kickball with the others. Would you like to come, George?"

George shook his head. After Jeremiah had walked away, George looked at me. "I'm sorry, Dodge. Are you mad at me?"

"For what?"

"Saying there's no God."

"Can't be mad at you for saying how you feel."

"Why'd this have to happen, Dodge?" George's voice cracked as he spoke. "Why? Why'd everyone have to die? Why're we living like this?"

"I don't know, little man. I wish I did."

Then, surprising me, George stood, walked over to me and climbed on my lap.

As mature as he tried to be, as grown up as he acted, George was just a boy. A scared little boy. I wrapped my arms tight around him and he rested his head on my chest.

"I can't bring back what we had," I said. "But I promise you I will do everything I can to make this life worth living for you."

"I know you will. I may not believe all that much in God, but I believe in you, Dodge," he said. "I believe in you."

I felt George's arms lock tighter as his words seared into my heart.

There was nothing more I could tell him. All I could do was hold him, because I really believed, at that moment, he needed that security more than anything.

34. FAYE

"Do you know what it's like to fail mankind?" Dr. Lewis asked, his first question as he closed the door to his office. He didn't ask it with any edge, nor his typical arrogance. I suppose, or so I thought, it was more of a rhetorical question.

I took a seat, and he walked around and leaned against the edge of his desk. "I'm not here to chastise you for making the decision you have made. I am not bringing you here to change your mind or threaten you. I am here to enlighten you."

It was hard to pay attention at first, because I'd started to hear gunshots outside, coming more and more frequently. Then, as he talked, all other noise faded.

"When this virus began it seemed so simple to fix and fight. In my arrogance, I knew I could be the one who cured it. Come up with not only a serum to fight it but an inoculation against ever catching it. That, of course, was when it hadn't touched our soil yet."

"Weren't you the one who cured it?" I asked.

"I was. But early on, too full of myself, I made mistakes. And then, like a puzzle, we overthought the problem, and the virus soon became unstoppable. I vowed to work day and night. What do you remember about the virus?"

"Not much. Before I slipped into the coma they were just warning people to be cautious, that many were getting it. And then I woke up three weeks later."

"What is the last date you remember before waking up?"

"April fifteenth."

Dr. Lewis nodded. "Our first patients began dying around the first week of April. And then they just kept dying and dying. I had been working on it while it was overseas. Long before it got here. Long before our first case at the end of March. Do you by any chance know anything about the first victims? You were conscious?"

"No." I shook my head. "I was drowning in my own grief."

"Ah. Eventually, so was I."

I glanced up to him.

"The first deaths, oddly, all came within hours of one another. An elderly couple in their early eighties. A woman in her thirties and two children, both ten. A family returning from an overseas extended cruise to Spain." He forced a smile and made eye contact. "They were my family. My parents, my wife and kids. Ironically, the man who held the knowledge to stop the virus watched helplessly as his family died. Died of a virus I was certain I could beat. But didn't. Do you know what I did after that?"

"I can assume you went to work twice as hard."

"No. I stopped. In fact, when I knew everyone that I loved had this highly contagious virus, I took off my mask, all protective equipment, and welcomed it. It didn't touch me. So I just slipped away and bothered with no one."

I stared down at my hands. "I know that feeling."

"I suppose you do. So ..." He exhaled. "More people died, time moved quickly, and after a couple weeks and begging from colleagues who had already taken the research as far as they could ..." Dr. Lewis chuckled, his voice full of emotion. "In fact, they had implemented this place. After that, fine, I went back to work on the virus." He held up a single finger. "One week. Maybe less. I cured it. It was as simple as I'd first thought. Had I not taken the time to hide away in anger, I could have saved millions. Millions. I ... failed mankind. Whether I really did or not, no reasoning can convince me otherwise. I failed. So I ask you, do you know what it's like to fail mankind? Because if you don't—you will. I don't say this maliciously, I say it honestly. Maybe not today. But you will. You chose not to carry the gender-altered embryos because you are not willing to get attached, have children again, whatever the case. But I assure you, like I was the answer to saving a good portion of this world, you are the answer to saving the species."

I shook my head. "You can't say that. I firmly believe there are other women."

"Do you know that for a fact? I thought someone else could take my burden as well. Even if there are other women, what's to say the baby will be immune to the virus? What's to say the baby will be a girl? Maybe nature has decided to eliminate us and only male children will be born without the aid of science. And if you are the only woman, what if suddenly there is a power failure and we lose the embryos, or worse, something happens to Dr. Chatham? Believe it or not, Faye, you are the answer. There might be others, but we don't know if they exist, if we can do for them what we can right now. And right now is the time to take advantage of the fact that you are an answer. Don't gamble like I did. Don't grow old and leave this world never knowing if you could have made a difference when we were given the chance to begin again. Because of my selfish decision we lost our population. Don't let your selfish decision end the line of what is left."

He delivered to me, in that office, a very strong argument for going ahead with the procedure. Words that were hard to ignore. Words that I heard, despite the fighting that had erupted outside the walls of the hospital.

By late evening I was locked in my apartment with not just one, but two guards inside with me. Farmer, one of the first soldiers I'd met, had returned at James' request.

He told me that civil unrest had erupted, that the seventy men from Division Five had enlisted the help of other divisions and were trying to storm the gates of Division One.

Why? Officially, I was told it was because they felt they were treated at a sub-standard level, that they wanted what Division One had. They claimed they lived in tent cities and were starving. No electricity. They were made to work with little reward. That was what they claimed.

Whether or not there was any truth to the way they lived, I didn't know. But Farmer believed the biggest bargaining tool was me. He believed they were trying to get in to get me. I was a woman; the leaders needed me and wanted me. If they had me, they could demand a life with better means. They would have a say in how they lived.

No one had to leak my presence; like James had feared, someone from Division Five was being treated at the hospital while I walked about freely.

I worried about Tyler, but was assured he was fine.

"We just need to keep you safe," Farmer said. "As odd as it sounds, they will try to get you."

"Am I that big of a bargaining chip?"

"You're the last woman."

It sounded like a warzone outside, not just civil unrest. My windows were blackened and I was kept in the center of the apartment.

"Farmer, what happens if they get close?"

"I have a few ideas. Any breach, we have to move you to a good spot. Hide you. Hiding you won't be hard, but getting you there will." He lifted the backpack he'd brought with him. "This is my idea. Faye, you need to consider it. For your safety, to protect you, we have to hide you in every way possible. That includes hiding *what* you are." He unzipped the bag and lifted a pair of hair clippers. "What do you say?"

It wasn't an easy decision, but it was one I had to make quickly. I'd known the day would come when I'd have to transform for my safety, and that day was here. Farmer pulled the rest of the items from the bag and, with his help, I began my transformation.

It was a good thing I did, because not half an hour later, men from Division Five broke the barricade and were on my street.

36. MAJOR JAMES REYNOLDS

September tenth. Taking a Chinook, we flew to Washington, DC, from an airbase close to Division Two. We landed on the lawn of the White House.

Flying over, we had seen survivor camps in the city. I'd been through many major cities in my journey to find Faye, but never had I seen so many survivors in one place. Not that there were hundreds, but there were a lot of camps with a lot of people.

It was a search and retrieve mission for documents and other personal items. An insane trip, in my opinion, but it was the president.

Upon landing, we learned that there was unrest involving Division Five back at COM Camp. They were making serious trouble as well as demands. I wasn't comfortable being so far away.

I was reminded quite clearly that no matter how much we tried to take control, restore order and civility, the country was possibly too far gone. This was reiterated by the squatters that had taken over the west wing of the White House.

We asked them to leave, but one man reminded us that the White House belonged to the people.

President Keene, an easygoing man, was hard put to argue. All he said was, "Let's just get what we need and leave at first light."

The squatters didn't bother with us much, other than asking if we had extra food.

"There's an entire damn city out there," I told them. "Go look for it."

"Major," the president scolded. "You will provide these people with the items we have and don't need."

That was the problem. Before the world went to shit, we all felt the need to provide, and in a sense, still did. What was it getting us?

That order pushed me to the verge of saying "The hell with it" and just moving on from the government camps.

By nightfall, communications we received over the radio had led me to realize I would not have much of a choice. Things had got worse. Rebels from Division Five had stormed Division One and looted and taken over Division Two. However, Farmer's quick thinking got Faye and a few others to the safe house, a place I had been preparing for days.

"There were deaths, Major," Farmer said over the radio. "It's not good. The safe house will only work for so long."

He was right—until and if we restored order, Faye wasn't safe. In fact, would she ever be?

At first light we pulled out. None of us had really got any rest, and for the first time the president truly showed anger at the situation.

I listened to him rant and rave on the flight, and all the while I just wanted to tell him that if he'd listened to the military personnel in the first place, none of it would have happened.

When the call went out, inviting the public inside the walls of the government compound, the general had warned it would cause problems. While it was the easiest way to find a surviving woman, it wasn't the logical way.

We ended up going out to search for her anyhow, leaving us with hundreds of less than desirable survivors who were angry, bitter, mourning and lacking any true motivation to live a productive life any longer.

They had lost everything. They had nothing more to lose, and they lived like it.

Rising smoke told us we had to find an alternative place to land. The airfield was destroyed, and there were fires burning everywhere.

I was informed things were partly under control. Division One was secure, but not without losses. A jeep rendezvoused with us at the alternative landing site and took us to Division One.

Multiple casualties was an understatement. Everywhere I looked there were burnt buildings, bodies being moved. The damaged hospital was packed with the injured.

I gave the order not to treat any rebels. As inhumane as it sounded, my men came first. Especially with only two doctors and limited medical staff.

Dr. Lewis had been moved to the safe house, but Dr. Barry Chatham had been killed.

Our geneticist. Our link to ending the path to extinction—dead.

After a heartbreaking briefing, I made my way to the safe house, which was located forty miles northwest. An inconspicuous exit from the highway led to a two-lane road, then I turned down a hidden, narrow dirt driveway. After a half-mile drive through the trees, the track ended at a gate. One of my men was stationed just inside.

I drove through and parked the jeep; the cool, fresh air coming off the ocean hit me immediately. I saw a soldier walking the beach with another right behind him.

I started down the path that led to the house, then paused. There was a swing set, and seeing it caused an ache in my chest. I just stood there for a moment, looking at it. I remembered the day I'd erected that swing set. It was before we moved into our dream house.

I was a man who feared very little, but at that moment, I feared going into the house. I'd never gone back inside. I was scared it would be difficult, and as I stood there in the yard, I realized I hadn't been wrong.

While preparing the house as a safe location, I never went alone. I'd always brought one of my men; he'd unload everything we'd brought and carry it in, and I'd stay outside. I had been to the house several times in the previous week, but this was the closest I'd gone to that swing set.

As I was gathering the courage to go inside and see Faye, another soldier emerged from the side door.

"Major." He snapped to attention.

"At ease. Where's Faye? Inside?"

He shook his head. "On the beach."

A part of me felt relieved that I didn't have to go inside. Not yet. "Thank you," I said, and after a last glance back at the swing set, I walked to the beach.

One of the soldiers I'd seen before was at the water's edge, walking back and forth. He looked carefree; why wasn't he watching Faye? I called out to him. "Soldier. Where is Faye?"

He turned around. I was breathless.

It was Faye. She wore a T-shirt tucked into camouflage pants, and her long hair wasn't just gone, it was shaved close to her head in what looked like a number-two buzz cut. I was relieved. If I hadn't known it was Faye, then neither would the rebels who sought her.

I saw her shoulders drop, and she hurried over to me.

"James." She threw her arms around me.

Instinctively, I returned the embrace. "Are you all right?"

"Yes. No." Her voice was weak. "It was horrible. They were escorting us out. Barry was shot. He was shot right next to me. And Tyler, I don't know where he is. We were looking and they rushed me out." Her head dropped.

"That's what I need to talk to you about."

Faye gasped. I could tell she barely contained a scream. "Oh God, he's dead."

"No." I shook my head. "He's not dead. But we have a situation. They got him. They have Tyler."

37. FAYE

I hated guns.

The hatred went back to my father and his death. I was only nine when he was accidentally shot by a friend. Dodge had tried to teach me while we were at my home, but I didn't even want to touch his gun. I knew about them, just hated them.

So when we had to leave the apartment in a rush and Farmer made me shoulder that M4, not only was I thrown off balance by the weight, but it pulled me down emotionally as well.

He said that since I was trying to look the part of a male soldier, I certainly wouldn't be moving about without a weapon.

The vest covered my breasts, the jacket—or cover, as they called it—hung too far down over my hand, and the combat helmet was loose.

I felt like a sloppy mess, and there was no way anyone would believe I was a man, let alone a soldier. But things moved fast, and we ran as partners rather than Farmer escorting me. I had confirmation that I looked like a man when we arrived at the hospital and Dr.

Chatham blasted Farmer, asking where I was. He didn't realize it was me until he stepped closer.

The plan was to get Tyler, both scientists and another doctor, then flee through the back of the hospital to the hidden jeep. But when we got to the hospital, chaos had already erupted. Getting to Tyler's room was like playing a video game, darting forward, back, staying close to the wall—all to discover Tyler was already gone.

The shrill sound of my voice was a calling card to the rebels, and they caught up to us as Farmer dragged me to the back door.

We were there, we were out. Barry was on my right, Dr. Lewis on my left, Farmer holding up the rear. He directed Dr. Lewis to go through first, with me between the two men.

Dr. Lewis pushed open the back door, and in that brief moment, I guess when Farmer stepped sideways to cover us, Barry was shot in the back of the head. But as important as he was, as much as I liked him, I couldn't even take a moment to acknowledge his death.

I barely had time to scream before Dr. Lewis yanked me hard to the waiting jeep, which was buried in the brush. There was already a driver waiting in it, and after zero hesitation we zipped through the night, leaving me in a state of shock over Barry's death and confusion regarding the fate of Tyler and Farmer.

The first news we received about what had happened came when James arrived at the safe house. Although other soldiers had shown up looking for safety, they knew no more than we did. Farmer arrived later; he had stayed back to help defend the hospital.

Dr. Lewis was an emotional mess. His cool exterior had crumbled in the aftermath. I suppose he was better friends with Barry than he'd wanted to admit. He sat in the house, looking at a photo album. I didn't stay inside; I sat on the covered back porch. I found it soothing, watching the ocean. After a while I went down to the beach, then spent some time walking back and forth between the water and the porch.

I was seated on the step, facing the beach, when James came out of the house and sat down next to me. He reached over and laid a hand on my wrist. His hand shook.

I looked at his trembling fingers, then up at him. "What's wrong?"

He shook his head. "Just dealing." He sighed. "No word yet. I'm gonna have to go back and find out exactly what they want to do with Tyler. Why they took him."

"Because of me?"

"More than likely."

"We'll get him back, right? We have to."

"We'll get him back," James said firmly. "But I don't think things will ever be the same again. There's been a lot of damage both to morale and property in Divisions One, Two and Five. Because of that, things will be shaken all over."

"Will they rebuild?"

"Yep. Maybe this time, they'll take more time. I know they were rushing to save people and give them hope, but they didn't think through how people would react, they didn't think through the human side. To me, that should have been planned out before the lights were put back in place. Some things can't be rebuilt. The research wing suffered a lot of damage."

"The cure?" I asked.

"We recovered that. Dr. Lewis will be able to recreate it, we hope, but we have to take him elsewhere to do so. The gender-altered embryos are done. The cases were burned. So even if you had changed your mind, it's too late now."

I glanced at my folded hands and said nothing.

"I have to tell you, Faye, this cutting off your hair, taking a male look—it was a brave thing."

My reaction probably wasn't one he expected. I laughed, tossing my head back. "Brave? I am so far from brave." I shook my head in disgust. "This whole thing made me take a really deep look at myself. I sat right here and did a lot of thinking."

"With all that thinking, how can you say that you aren't brave?'

"Because I'm not. I'm afraid. I'm weak. I've been living in some stupid fantasy world, thinking that all will be okay because I let everyone else handle things for me."

"Faye …"

"No, James, it's true. When I got up from that mound of bodies, physically I was sick, but emotionally I was strong. I was determined to make it home and die. Then I met Dodge, and I just handed the responsibility to him. He'd get me home, he'd help find food. I didn't worry about anything too much because Dodge handled everything. And here I sit, waiting on Dodge, waiting on you, so I can feel safe and better. That's not the way it should be. I should be able to do everything within my physical capabilities. Poor Dodge, the responsibility I put on him."

"In your defense…"

I laughed.

"No, listen." He held up a hand. "You need more protection than you can give yourself. You are a commodity that is sought in this world. And like any commodity, food, water, gas, it takes a team to keep it secure until things straighten out, if they ever do. One person cannot protect the whole gas supply. You alone cannot constantly protect yourself."

"But I should know how. Dodge tried to teach me." I shrugged. "I blew it off. I figured he can shoot people. Hell, Farmer weaponized me and I balked."

James laughed. "Weaponized you?"

"Yeah, put a rifle here, pistol there, that sort of thing. I couldn't touch them. I felt sloppy, and that I would hurt the wrong person."

"Farmer told me about your opposition to guns."

"I have to get over it. I have to at least be able to protect myself if Dodge isn't there."

"I know. I have something for you." He grabbed my hand. "You cannot effectively protect yourself if you are intimidated by the weapon you hold. Let's face it, an M4 is heavy and intimidating. A nine-millimeter is too. This should not intimidate you."

James placed what I thought was a toy revolver in my hand. It couldn't have been any more than four inches, with a tiny trigger and a tiny hammer.

"It's loaded, so be careful."

"It's real?"

"Oh, yeah." He took the revolver, holding it gently. "A twenty-two Magnum—not the smallest made, but close. Barrel ejects up for easy load. It's a single-action trigger, which means you have to cock it back before you shoot." He cocked it, aimed and then gently replaced the hammer. "I'm gonna tell you, it's not good at distances. But close up it is—perfect if you get yourself in a tight spot. It's a starter gun, and it shouldn't scare you." He placed it in my hand. "It can save you."

"Like when those guys grabbed me."

"Yep." He set a box of ammunition on the porch. "Take today. Learn how to use it. Be Dirty Harry." He smiled. "It sounds like a firecracker and it's not real loud. Will you practice?"

I looked down at the weapon.

"Please. You say you want to be strong. Protect yourself. You can only do that if you learn. I'll assign a soldier to work with you. Just have it with you and don't let the kids see it, because they'll think it's a toy."

My only reply was a nod. I felt the weapon in my hand. I wasn't intimidated by it. "Are you leaving?"

"I have to head back to base. You're fine here. I'll check back if I can. But more than likely not—I don't want to be followed."

"Thank you for this. What did you do, stop at a gun shop?"

James laughed. "No, that was my wife's. I got it for her because she hated guns and I wanted her to have something she was comfortable with."

I was shocked; James had spoken about his fear of going back to his house. "You went home?"

"I did." He nodded.

"See. You didn't need me there."

"I wouldn't exactly say that."

I gave him a curious look.

He turned his head, looked at the house and waved his hand. "Mine."

I gasped. "Oh, James—this is your house?"

He nodded. "When I prepared it, I didn't step inside. Going in for this gun was the first time I went in since the virus hit. It was hard. But I had good motivation."

"Your photo albums? Pictures? This was your life?" I reached over and grabbed his arm. "This is wonderful. I love it here. I don't even want to leave. Ever."

"Unfortunately, staying isn't an option. Not yet. Maybe one day you can come back here. But until we deal with the problems, until we can make life normal and safe for you and any other female, remote is best."

"Baby steps to normality?"

"Baby steps to normality," he said. "First one being, we get Tyler back."

Listening to James, I got the feeling that I wouldn't be hiding forever. Just as I was taking steps to keep myself safe, so was he. I loved the beach house, and I wanted to make it my goal to return there.

Something inside told me James was going to make that a goal as well. His job before the virus was to fight to make the world a better and safer place; no doubt he was still doing his job.

38. DODGE

A sickening feeling hit my gut when I saw the smoke rising up in the distance. Though I wasn't certain it was from the government camp, my instincts said it was.

We were still twenty miles north of the place, and I stopped.

Thank God, no pun intended, Deacon Jeremiah had made the trip. Since we'd left the RV, intending to return right away, he'd traveled with us "just in case."

This was one of those "just in case" moments.

"You got twenty miles," Jeremiah said. "It should not take you long to get there, find out what happened, if anything, and return for us. I think it's safer for me and the boys to hang back in case there is trouble."

Hating to do so, I agreed.

"No," George argued. "We need to see Faye and Tyler."

"You will. Let me make sure everything is good."

Jeremiah asked, "What do you think happened?"

"Could be something as simple as a house fire, or something like a raid by survivors."

Jeremiah looked around. "See that speed limit sign?" He pointed back. "We'll be in the wooded area. If need be we can retreat and run to the house not far down the road. But we haven't seen anyone, so I feel safe."

"Don't take this the wrong way, but are you able to handle trouble?"

Jeremiah smiled. "I'm protected. I have God in my heart … and a thirty-eight in my jacket."

"You're carrying?"

"Brother Daniel said God leads but man has free will, and in circumstances such as this, you can't trust what that free will is going to do."

I looked back at the smoke. How right he was.

After making sure they were hidden and safe, I got back in the car. I hadn't made it ten miles before I got to two big military trucks blocking the road. Fifteen feet away, I was ordered to stop by the armed soldiers standing around them.

As if I wasn't going to do that.

One soldier approached the car, and I was so grateful the boys weren't with me. I lifted my hands in the air.

"Step out of the vehicle slowly," he said.

I opened the door, lifted my hands again and stepped out. "Look, I'm just heading to the camp. My family is there. If you don't mind, this cast is heavy and I'd rather not hold my arms up too long."

He nodded. "Your family is in which camp?"

"There's more than one?" I asked, shocked. "I don't know. I have two little boys waiting about ten miles back with a friend. I am here to find my son and—"

I stopped.

"And?"

"And you're probably not going to believe this. But … the woman. Faye."

The soldier stepped back. "Major," he called out. "Major, can you come here, please, sir."

A man of average height and build got out of the front of one of the trucks and started walking my way. After a moment he slowed down, tilting his head, then picked up the pace.

"Major, this man says—"

"Are you Dodge?" he asked.

"Yes, I am." I couldn't keep the surprise out of my voice.

"Wow. Last I saw you, you were down and out on the ground."

"Thank you for that."

"James." He held out his hand. "James Reynolds."

The soldier said, "Is this the guy you were talking about?"

"Yes." James nodded. "Where are the boys? Is everything all right?"

"I left them back with my friend. I saw the smoke."

Another soldier had approached. "Hey!" he said, upbeat. "Dodge. You are doing great. You were really messed up when I worked on you."

"Thank you both for reminding me how bad I got my ass kicked." I paused. "And thank you on a serious note for helping us. Now— where's Faye and Tyler?"

They all looked at each other, then back at me. I could tell the news wasn't going to be good.

James, the major and a man who went by the name Farmer drove me back to the road to get Jeremiah and the boys. We didn't say anything to them, just that Faye had been moved to a really cool spot.

James had filled me in on the way. He told me someone had given the rebels all the information they needed, and they knew that without Faye, the government couldn't complete Project Eve. According to James, the rebellion had screwed it all up.

He told me how they'd wanted Faye to get pregnant with girls. A chance, if only a small one, to jump-start things. I didn't tell them about the women at the monastery. It wasn't my place to do so.

The rebels had my son. They also had suicide bombers ready to destroy not only the hospital, but the grid and water supply as well.

James said, "I don't care about the grid. I do care about the hospital. All the research is there."

He didn't say much more, nor did he go into his plan in any detail; he told me he would once we were with Faye. He also assured me that he had taken great care to watch her and make sure she was safe.

I'd be lying if I said a bit of jealousy didn't creep up inside me.

In fact, I stewed over it until we arrived at the safe house. Then all those feelings seemed to vanish. The boys and I got out of the car, with Jeremiah behind us, and we had just made it past the swing set when I spotted Faye.

No one had told me she had shaved her head and dressed like a man. It didn't work for me. I knew even at a distance it was her, standing there at the edge of the water.

So did the boys. They flew by me, screaming her name at the top of their lungs.

"Faye! Faye!"

I walked on, watching them run to her. She spun around, her face lighting up, and hurried to the boys. They both plowed into her so hard, they knocked her back and she dropped to her knees. It was an amazing reunion, and I wanted to be a part of it.

At first I believed she was so preoccupied with the boys that I was an afterthought. Then, with Darie and George in her arms, she looked up. The biggest smile I ever saw graced her face. She kissed both boys, stood, chuckled and ran to me. The boys followed her and sandwiched themselves between us, grasping our legs as I did my best just to hold on to her.

It felt so good to see her, to hold Faye and know she was fine. She looked absolutely fine.

"I am so happy to see you guys." She squeezed tightly and then pulled back. "How are you? I was so worried about you. But I knew inside you'd be fine."

"I'm good. How are you?"

"Physically fine. Tyler …"

I held up my hand. "I know."

"I'm sorry. I am so sorry."

"This isn't your fault."

Then her expression changed, and I knew it was the moment I'd been dreading. Faye shifted her eyes, looking about. "Where's Bud?"

A lump formed in my throat, and the words were hard to say. "We lost Bud. He … passed away two days ago."

Her hand shot to her mouth and she gasped. "Oh no." Then she cringed, almost as though the news had made her nauseous. "Please tell me he wasn't beat up, or shot, or suffered."

I shook my head. "No, he passed away in his bed in the RV. In his sleep."

Faye nodded a few times, then let out a slow sigh. She lifted Darie to rest on her hip, such a motherly gesture, and brought George closer. "Then I'm glad he went that way. Was he happy? Did he say anything?"

"He was confident that we would find you."

George peered up at her. "We had a funeral. They put him in a coffin like my grandpa. Had music in the church and everything."

"A funeral?" she asked.

"I'll explain it to you later, just …" I pointed at Jeremiah, who had held back behind us.

"Is he Amish? Was it an Amish town? He has that beard and hair …"

I laughed. "No, he's a monk."

"I see," Faye murmured.

But I don't think she did. Our reunion on that beach was brief. And it took everything we had to get the boys away from the ocean. I promised them they could play there when Tyler got back. They agreed and came to the house.

"They want to meet," James said as we stood on the back porch. "One hour. Two of us and the woman, two of them and Tyler. I set the meet at an open spot where they can't bring anyone to ambush us. They said once the exchange is made, they will call off their guys at the grid, water supply and hospital and negotiate in good faith. Right now, I have snipers on the suicide bombers, ready to take them out on my call."

"What's the plan?" I asked.

"Take them out, get Tyler and give the call, and then we storm Division Two to break them there." James nodded briefly. "That's the plan."

"Sounds too easy."

"We're not dealing with rocket scientists or organized terrorist cells. We're dealing with outraged and irrational human beings. They tend not to think things through."

"Good. When do we go?" I asked.

"We?" James shook his head. "You don't go. We do."

"What! That is my son."

"And I will do everything I can to ensure I deliver your child back to you. Trust me. But if something goes wrong … Those boys in there. Those little boys need you."

I chuckled in disbelief. "If something goes wrong they'll have Faye."

James didn't say anything. His silence told me a lot.

"No." I shook my head. "You're taking Faye?"

"They said two men and the woman. There will be two men and Faye."

"Unbelievable. You're gonna use her as bait? Pretend you're handing her over?"

"I'm taking her. I need her there, just in case they ask to hear her voice. None of us sound female enough to pull it off. They can make things go bad quickly if they know it's a ruse. But she's not the woman I'm handing over." The screen door behind me squeaked. James nodded at it and I turned around.

Farmer, who was only about two inches taller than Faye and thinner, walked onto the porch. He was wearing that scarf or bandana Faye always wore, and dangling over his shoulder was a ponytail. It was Faye's hair, from when she'd cut it. He also wore her tan shorts and that pink T-shirt that irritated me because it made her stand out when she should have been camouflaged.

Faye sighed. "He wears that so much better than me."

I shot a quick glance at Faye, then back to Farmer. I could tell immediately she was envious. Not because Farmer wore it better, but because he wore it at all and she was dressed like a man. It had come to the point where the world was forcing her to hide her femininity.

"Now do you see the plan?" James asked.

I groaned. I saw the plan, but I didn't like it. What choice did I have?

Faye's goodbye to the boys was short and sweet, as though she were going to the grocery store. We didn't want them to worry. She briefly met Jeremiah; there wasn't time for long introductions or explanations about where he came from.

James and the very feminine Farmer were in the jeep, Farmer in the back. Faye was ready to go, but before she stepped from the porch, I gave her a once over. It was hard to believe it was her. The strap from her helmet added a thickness to her chin. It looked too heavy for her. The uniform was slightly too big, and the sleeves on the jacket nearly buried her hands.

"Be careful out there," I said.

"Tyler will be fine."

"I know he will. You … be careful."

"I promise."

"I'm a nervous wreck, Faye. You shouldn't be doing this."

"Yeah, Dodge, I should." She spoke softly. "I have to. I don't expect you to understand. But I need to just take charge of my destiny, even if it's only one moment."

"I understand."

"When I come back, will you tell me about this place that gave our friend a real funeral?"

"I will. But now your chariot awaits."

As Faye took a step forward, I stopped her once more and embraced her. Embracing Faye was natural. I'd lost count of how often we'd hugged over the months, or huddled close while George read to us. I didn't realize how much I missed it until it wasn't there.

Now, after being separated, she was trudging into dangerous territory. I was scared.

Placing my hand on the side of her face, I leaned forward and kissed her. Fast enough not to annoy her and soft enough to let her know, "Hey, I care and I'm here waiting and worrying."

She smiled tightly, and as she walked by me she said, "That was nice." She paused before getting in the jeep. "I was wondering when you would ever try that."

A small laugh escaped, along with some sort of post-kiss teenage twinge. That was quickly replaced with worry as I watched them drive off.

39. FAYE

Without much hair, I could feel the beads of sweat forming on my head under the heavy helmet. My stomach fluttered with nerves.

"If it goes the way I hope," James said as he drove, "this will be over in three minutes. We're meeting at the old Big Shop's parking lot; they tore the building down to make room for a tent city. Nothing is there. They should be there now, but I'll park at a distance. I'll propose one of them brings Tyler as I escort Farmer. I'll try to keep the pacing even with their man. I don't want to get too close or they'll know Farmer is a man. Once we've passed them and they are clear of us, I need you to cough."

"Cough?" I asked.

"Once if they move to my left. Twice if they are directly behind me. And three times"—James demonstrated—"like that if they veer right. We have one shot. When you cough, you get down. I will turn around to take out the man with Tyler and at the same time Farmer will take out the man in front of us."

"What if there are men hidden?"

"That's possible. If gunfire erupts, take cover under the jeep. But where we are meeting, there's nowhere close to hide. I don't think they're bringing anyone. They won't think it's an ambush."

"I think you're underestimating them. I think they're gonna pull something. This is too easy."

Farmer reached up and gripped my shoulder. "We got this."

I glanced at the fingernail polish. "Why am I wearing a nice shirt and fingernail polish?"

"Because they know, or at least think, you were pampered. We're just banking on their preconceived notion of what they think a woman would do."

When we arrived, I could see the parking lot from the road. Fallen tents were rolling along and dancing in the wind. There was a blue pickup truck center of the lot, and James pulled in and stopped a good hundred feet away. He put the jeep in park but left the engine running, and he and I got out.

Two men climbed out of the truck, hauling Tyler with them. "Well, don't I feel honored," the older man called. "Got the major himself."

"Tyler, you okay?" James yelled.

"Yes."

"I see pink," the rebel shouted. "Let me hear her talk."

Both James and I faced Farmer. When my back was to the men, I raised my voice. "Tyler, it will be all right."

The leader laughed. "Well, send her over."

"No," James said. "Even exchange. Same time. You bring him, we bring her to you. Let's end this shit."

"I couldn't agree more, Major."

James reached into the jeep to assist Farmer. Farmer kept his arms tight to his body, as if cold or upset; I knew he was concealing a small handgun.

"Not you," the man yelled. "The smaller soldier. Have him bring the woman."

My eyes widened, and James looked at me with a wince. He lowered his voice. "Okay, change up. Get ready to hit the deck, Faye. When I shoot, Farmer will take out that asshole."

I nodded.

"Don't worry," James said.

"I'm not." I stayed close to Farmer as we moved in front of the jeep.

My heart raced with each step we took. Midway, Tyler and the other man passed us. I made brief eye contact with him.

It was the longest walk of my life, and as we drew closer, I noticed the sawn-off shotgun in the leader's hand. It was aimed at me, and I realized they were planning the same thing.

They were going to shoot me at the same time they shot James.

We were getting closer. Why hadn't James fired? At ten feet the leader commanded, "Stop."

We did. I eyed the shotgun and knew it was coming.

"Don't take that boy any closer," the leader said to the other man.

I glanced over my shoulder, fast enough to see Tyler was the same distance from James as I was from the leader.

Or so I thought.

When I turned back around, the leader was only a few feet away, and the shotgun was even closer to my chest. He raised it with a smile and looked at Farmer. "Aren't you a pretty thing?"

Come on, James, shoot, I thought. *Do something.* Why wasn't James shooting? Was the gun on Tyler?

"What's your name?" the leader asked Farmer. "Fanny? Faye?"

Farmer's head was down.

"Doesn't matter."

Had I known better, maybe I would have seen that the shotgun was already engaged.

251

At a distance of only four feet, the leader fired. The blast was so powerful it shattered Farmer's chest. I felt his blood splatter onto me as the noise crashed against my eardrums like thunder.

I don't even believe I screamed, I was in such a state of shock.

A high humming filled my ears and everything seemed to move in slow motion. Farmer's body dropped to the ground and my knees buckled.

I didn't have time to panic or even feel scared. I knew running was my only option. I spun to my right, saw the other rebel on the ground and James running my way.

I never heard the shot from James.

The leader grabbed my left arm. I struggled and fought to get free. My hearing came back some, enough to hear the man yelling at James.

"Stay back!"

I glanced back; James had stopped, and I saw Tyler in the jeep. In that moment I took to look, I stopped struggling for a split second and the leader pulled me back.

No, I thought, *this is not happening again.*

I brushed into him. Because he was holding the shotgun, he could only grip me by my left arm.

"Come any closer and I'll shoot her. I don't care," he shouted to James. "Not anymore."

He yanked me nearer. That was when I really looked at him, looked into his eyes. I saw nothing. His expression blank, he was a man without emotions, a man on the edge. He really wasn't afraid to take my life.

Maybe that had been his intention all along.

Not to have me, but to kill me. Kill me out of bitterness, because he believed I was the last woman.

His top lip twitched and he stared at me. For some reason I lost all fear. Was this what remained of our world? Was this man a representation of what I had to run from for the rest of my life? Or were he and his kind just exceptions to the rule that man would rise above barbaric tendencies?

All these thoughts consumed me in just the few seconds that we were locked in that stare.

"Your buddy's dead."

"So is yours," I said.

He laughed. "You think I care?" He shook his head. "You think I didn't know you were the woman? Did you think I was stupid?"

"Yes." As I said that single word, I thumbed back the hammer on the mini twenty-two Magnum concealed in my hand beneath the too-big sleeves of my jacket. Without hesitation, my eyes still locked on his, I lifted the revolver to his chin and fired.

He never saw it coming.

For a moment I swore he knew that bullet entered his brain. The tiny gun had just enough power to end his life, and with one last blink of his eyes he registered his death.

His grip released. I stepped out of the way and his body fell to the ground.

Tyler cried out, "Oh my God, Faye." I heard footsteps as he and James ran to me.

All I could think about was Farmer. I dropped to my knees next to him, grabbing his lifeless hand in mine. His eyes were open, and I closed them. I prayed that he had felt nothing and had died instantly. I felt bad, truly bad. He hadn't deserved his death sentence.

"Faye." Tyler knelt down. "Are you okay?"

I nodded.

"Faye," James said. "I'm—"

"What was his first name?" I asked, looking at Farmer.

"I'm sorry? What—"

"What was his first name? Everyone called him Farmer. What was his first name?"

"It was … something odd," James stuttered, clearly struggling to think. "Blain. His first name was Blain."

"Thank you. I just needed to know that."

I stayed with him for a while longer. I owed him that much. The brave and brilliant young man had saved Tyler's life once before, and now had given his own to save him again.

For that I would be forever grateful. I would always hold a special place in my heart for Lieutenant Blain Farmer.

40. MAJOR JAMES REYNOLDS

The beat-up blue pickup had enough gas for me to return to base. I gave Faye and Tyler directions to get back to the safe house. I also radioed on the secure channel for one of my men to be on the road.

I honored the motto to "leave no man behind," and in all my years in the service, I never had. I wasn't going to start now.

Farmer was the first soldier I'd watched die in the post-virus world. His death hit me hard. It would never be forgotten or in vain.

He was a casualty in a new war. The first battle had raged.

It wasn't over. Not by a long shot. We had successfully taken out the threats at the grid, water system and hospital, but we still had many more.

I recognized the man Faye had shot. He was one of the leaders in Division Five. I didn't know if the others were dead or were actively looking for their next move.

Even if Faye's theory about the men wanting her just to kill her were true, it wouldn't be long before they would want her because she was a woman. That alone was a problem.

We had not fortified COM Camp as well as we had believed. We were fine until we brought in a commodity that someone wanted. For the time being, even with rebel leaders still in control and still plotting, I believe we had scattered them enough to buy some time.

Not much, though.

Wherever Faye and her family went, it would have to be safe and secure. None of us really knew what it was like west of Texas. I hoped traveling that far wasn't part of their plan.

No matter where they went, I needed to know. I needed to be there to back them up, to be able to check on her, because if indeed she was the last woman, she was precious and it would be every man's responsibility to preserve that.

The last thing I wished for Faye was a life of hiding and fear. And after what I'd witnessed, after seeing her take her fate in her own hands, Faye wouldn't live in fear.

She rose from the depths of a pile of dead flesh, and had changed from a person who just wanted to die to a woman who fought to live.

I envied that.

There's more to life than just breathing, and like Faye, one day I too hope to experience that.

One day.

41. DODGE

It was the hardest wait I had ever experienced. I wagered on it being several hours. I didn't expect to hear the jeep return so quickly.

There were two porches at the beach house. One faced the ocean, the other faced the driveway. We all sat on that front wraparound porch, waiting and hoping for the best.

As well as me, Jeremiah and the boys, there were also four soldiers, Dr. Lewis and a senator, who didn't say much. I was shocked to learn the president had survived, and more so that he wasn't at the safe house.

Three people went out to get my son. When the jeep came up the driveway and I only saw two figures, my stomach dropped.

My heart sank and thumped in my stomach when I saw my son step from the jeep.

I was already out and unconscious when they took him south for help. I never saw how badly injured he was, but the boy that raced toward me looked healthy and only a little thinner.

"Dad!" He sounded so enthusiastic, so relieved, and that made me ever so grateful. I leaped from the porch to greet him with the biggest embrace.

I looked past him and saw Faye. I let out a deep breath and reached out my hand. "I am so glad you two are safe. So glad." I planted my lips to my son's cheek, holding them there for a few seconds.

"Dad, you should have seen." Tyler stepped back. "I think the outfit and haircut made Faye—"

Faye shook her head and Tyler stopped talking. Obviously something had happened that she didn't want me to know about. I didn't force the issue.

Faye would tell me in time. She held nothing back from me.

"Where's James and Farmer?" I asked.

Faye's face fell and she looked up at the sky. It was obvious she was trying not to cry. "Farmer was killed. James had to return to base. He'll be back." She slid her hand over my arm and walked to the porch.

My arm around Tyler, I followed.

On the porch, she announced to everyone that Farmer had been shot. He had seemed like a good man, and it was apparent from everyone's reactions that he would be sorely missed.

"What now?" Dr. Lewis asked.

Faye shrugged. "I don't know. James seems to think we're okay now, but not for long."

"Then we pack up and go," I said. "We take the boys and go. We need to find a place to settle."

"You need to find a stable and safe place for her," Dr. Lewis interjected. "She can't run constantly."

"What about you?" Faye asked him. "Where are you going?'

"I have research to start again. It's a focus I welcome."

Then George blurted out, "What about Monk Land, Faye? You still have to go there."

"Monk Land?" Faye asked.

"That's what Dodge calls it," George said.

"Oh, I do not. Stop telling tales."

"You called it that."

"Once."

Jeremiah cleared his throat. "If I may? George is speaking about Holy Cross Monastery. That's where I come from. Your friend Bud liked it there. He hoped that you'd go there and stay. We are embedded very deeply in the mountains. A huge wall protects our entrance and we also have guards. We have water, greenhouses, livestock and a doctor."

Faye looked at Dr. Lewis, who asked, "Is it a real doctor? Not some backwoods or herbal healing person?"

"He was the town doctor. We have a community," Jeremiah said. "People living there. Starting life again."

Faye looked at me. "Dodge? What do you think of this place?"

"Honestly?"

"No less."

"I want us to go somewhere and start fresh. But it offers the safety you need and the freedom you deserve."

Her eyes shifted about and she grabbed my hand. "Are there children there? I want Darie and George to grow up around kids."

"There are kids there." I leaned close to her and whispered in her ear. "And women."

Her eyes brightened and she looked at Jeremiah. "Then we go. It sounds perfect for now."

"Plus," George said, "Bud is there. We can go see him any time."

"There is a problem," Jeremiah said. "A good portion of the town retreated to our mountain haven. They are not immune to the virus."

"We have a vaccine now," Dr. Lewis said. "Many of the people down here were given it. If you'll welcome it, we'll bring it."

"Yes," Jeremiah said excitedly, and extended his hand to Dr. Lewis. "Without a doubt. We want to preserve any and all life that we can. We have to make sure life goes on."

"Then we have the same agenda," Dr. Lewis replied.

There was an odd sense of resolution in that moment. A much appreciated reunion; those I cared about were alive and well.

Bud would have loved that moment. Probably would have even spewed out a sarcastic comment that it was turning into a happy ending after all. Thinking about Bud made me smile. I guess I looked pretty goofy, because I got a bunch of strange glances.

For the first time in a long time, deep in my gut, I truly felt everything was going to be just fine. Never the same, never the way it was, but fine nonetheless.

I could live with that.

42. FAYE

We were told we had a couple days to enjoy the house until we had to leave. James was certain there was a safety time frame, and Dr. Lewis needed a day or two to get the vaccine packed. Because they didn't want to take the chance of being followed or anything happening on the road, they were preparing a helicopter to take us to West Virginia. I was good not having to make that long drive.

But I did look forward to spending that alone time with Dodge and the boys. The evening after we were all reunited, it felt normal. It was absolutely perfect.

None of the boys, including Tyler, wanted to leave that beach. After dinner they played there for hours. Football, sand castles, whatever they could do.

Dodge and I sat on the steps of the back porch, watching the three of them laughing and darting about. The sun was setting and the moment was just serene.

I slipped my fingers between Dodge's. I'd forgotten how much I missed holding his hand, sitting there with him, stealing our evening moments as we'd done so many times since we first met.

"I wish we didn't have to leave here," I said. "This house is great."

"Yeah, it is. Maybe we can come back one day. Maybe one day things will be good again."

"Do you think?"

"Yeah, I do. You're not the only one, Faye. So there are more. Even if you are few and far between, there will be a time when it's gonna be okay to move about."

"And smell like purple soap again?"

"You smell like it now."

I sniffed my arm and shrugged. "They let me use it. Of course, I don't need my shampoo. Regular soap works now."

Dodge reached over and rubbed my buzzed head. "It kinda works for you."

"Really."

"Yeah. I like it. Now I don't have to worry about finding your hair in my food."

That made me laugh, and then so did the sight of Tyler with Darie in the water. "Be careful," I called, the mother in me coming out.

"So," Dodge said, "COM Camp was nice?"

"Where they had me was. But it doesn't beat this.

"Really now? You had a fridge, hot water, air-conditioning. You think this is better?"

"Wherever we all are is better. Don't get me wrong, I wouldn't mind having all this and the running water." I nudged him and then rested my head on his arm. "But there really is no choice in my mind."

"Thank you." He kissed the top of my head. "So, uh, James told me about why they wanted you. Project Eve."

I lifted my head.

"Something wrong?" he asked.

"I forgot. For a brief moment, I really forgot."

"About Project Eve?"

"Yes." I nodded.

"Well, according to James, that's out. The lab was destroyed."

I turned to face him properly. "What did you think of that? I mean, them wanting me to carry female babies."

"I saw their reasoning. They believed you were the last woman, and by impregnating you with girls, they were making sure you weren't."

"Kind of pointless now, right?"

"No. More like moot. The project is over. The thought of it is. Now it's up to nature. Until then"—Dodge pulled me closer—"we have our little family." He winked and nodded at the boys. "I'm happy with what we have."

"Me too."

We fell into a peaceful silence, watching the boys. They only had a few more minutes of light, then we'd have to go in. No fires, no outside light. We still had to take precautions.

I thought about Project Eve and how I wanted to tell Dodge. I wanted to tell him that Dr. Lewis had delivered a heartfelt argument, and that at some point, listening to him say that the embryos could be accidentally destroyed, and listening to the gunfire, I had suddenly decided leaving it to fate wasn't a gamble I wanted to take.

Yes, I wanted to leave it up to nature, but there was no certainty that I would get pregnant, let alone carry a girl. The cases of gender-altered embryos had been an assurance that the female species would live on. Call it a hunch, or even female intuition—whatever it was, I'd changed my mind.

And before I could change it again, before the rebels stormed the hospital, we had gambled that the single dose of fertility preparation would work.

Five female embryos were implanted in me not even eight hours before those cases were destroyed.

Whether the in vitro had worked remained to be seen. There was a chance our little family was going to get bigger. Until I knew for sure whether it had taken hold, I'd stay mum on the subject.

I stopped short of telling Dodge about it all. I wanted to, I really did. Instead I opted to sit there and just enjoy the fact that we were all back together again.

With the possibility that I was in fact with child, watching the boys on the beach and holding Dodge's hand, I couldn't ask for a clearer sign that no matter what, life finds a way. And it goes on.

EPILOGUE - FAYE

FIVE YEARS LATER

WAYNE, WV

It was time to leave the nest. At least, that was the way Tyler put it when work on the town of Wayne was complete. Of course, Tyler had left our nest not long after we returned to Holy Cross. He had bonded with Jeremiah and decided to study under the monks.

He claimed he wasn't a monk, and nor would he ever take that route, but somehow he gained a focus through his studies, and he began to create art that was truly remarkable.

I believe the solace of the monastery was what Tyler liked best. That and the peace. They gave him a single cabin near the main building.

While Dodge worked hard getting things running and finding a way to restore partial power, I learned the fine art of making soap. That doesn't sound like much or an impressive resume, but it was a craft I learned there and one I enjoyed doing. I'd never had a skill like that. Tyler would often carve molds for me, and always, the soaps I made for myself were purple.

Over the first two years, survivors trickled in. Around year three, they just stopped.

But our community grew, which was one of the reasons Dodge and the others worked so hard on Wayne.

The second we walked into Holy Cross on that first day, I knew I was home. It was a perfect community, and it reminded me of what I'd read about pilgrims. Dodge insisted we weren't going to be there long.

Eight months after we arrived, I gave birth early to a beautiful set of twin girls. I had carried triplets until my fifth month, but lost one.

Dr. Lewis showed up not long after I lost the first baby, and he never left. He was one of the first people to move back to Wayne after Dodge and the others completed work on the first street.

Darie and George grew up as normally as the world let them. They read and wrote stories and played games without relying on gadgets or gizmos. They had been ready to move into Wayne long before me. I'd found security behind the walls of Holy Cross, a safety blanket that took five years to lose.

James dismantled COM Camp and then began the task of rebuilding it. We communicate with them regularly, and James stops by every three months. He's doing well and staying busy.

Dr. Lewis says that technically I am still the only woman to have survived the virus. The women at Holy Cross weren't immune. The vaccine assured their survival, because the virus was still going strong.

Other threats have emerged, and Dr. Lewis works hard to fight them. Whooping cough came back with a vengeance, and all the inoculations we had had already expired.

Since the virus, eight babies have been born, including my daughters. One child died of whooping cough. Of the seven that live, my babies are the only girls.

I worried whether I would even like the girls. Would I feel for them like I did Sammy and Mark? Would I love them like I loved Tyler, Darie and George? After all, biologically they weren't mine. I doubted there'd even be a connection.

But when they were born, all doubts went out the window. They were my children. No, they were mine and Dodge's children. I never expected him to be less than a great father, and that's exactly what he is. The day we baptized the twins, two years to the day since I woke up on that field of dead bodies, I started a new chapter of my life and married Dodge.

We made our little family—or rather big family—official. We didn't need to, but we wanted to.

I stopped letting Dodge do everything for me and went back to my old self-sufficient ways—though I made one exception to that rule. Diaper duty.

The day I left Holy Cross reminded me of the day I left for college. I was sad and scared; after all, I was leaving a home I'd had for five years.

It was a big change and a big step. But in our new life, that's what everything was—new.

Life wasn't the same as it was before the virus wiped out the world we knew. It never will be.

We take it as it comes. One step at a time, one day at a time.

We close our eyes at night and sleep peacefully. We wake up grateful to be facing another day. Considering the tremendous heartache behind us and the painful memories we carry, I'd say we're doing okay.

We couldn't ask for any more. We're still alive, and not only that—we're living.

ABOUT THE AUTHOR

Jacqueline Druga is a native of Pittsburgh, PA. Her works include genres of all types but she favours post-apocalypse and apocalypse writing.

You can find more of her books at www.vulpine-press.com

Follow the author on Facebook @jacquelinedruga

Visit her website www.jacquelinedruga.com